CW00408645

STONE RUSH

A Stone Cold Thriller

J.D WESTON

1

SINKING HEART

IN THE DARKNESS OF THE NIGHT, THE CALM, INKY-BLACK waters of the Mediterranean offered Bella one of very few choices.

She peered over the side of the boat as the water gently licked at the wooden hull below, and listened to the slurp and splash of the water as the vessel met the oncoming tide.

Bella searched ahead into the night for a sign of the first option: Greece. She'd been told that when the mountains appeared on the horizon, her journey would be coming to an end. But that did not guarantee her safety or the safety of her unborn child; even *she* knew that. A new journey would begin with new dangers, but it would be a journey of hope.

Behind her, Turkey had long since disappeared from sight, taking Bella's only friend, Yana, with it; there may be a a chance that Bella could return, but it was very slim.

Yana and Bella had travelled from Syria together, huddled in the back of a truck under heavy canvasses that smelled of oil, dirt and urine. That seemed an age ago, when Bella had had only two options: stay and be killed or leave and head into the unknown. Their chances of survival as the pair had begun their journey from Aleppo had been very small but they had made it, just.

Bella wished Yana had joined her on the boat. She wished that someone had answered her prayers, but the greed and lust of man had been no match for the two young girls.

As children, Yana had always been the prettier of the two, although she'd downplayed it, and had always told Bella that she would meet a great man who would care for her and provide her with many children. But Yana's fair skin and large, clear eyes had steered her away from Bella in the end. Their journey had been fraught with danger and controlled by men along the way. The two girls had merely been garbage floating in the sea, this way and that, pulled by the tides of cruel men and pushed by their will to survive.

Bella knew that they would never meet again.

In front, somewhere in the darkness, lay the uncertainty of another journey by road, through Europe and finally to England, where she had been told she would be welcomed, fed and sheltered. Behind her was certain death, but the chance to see her friend one last time.

Bella's third option lay beneath her. It was the easiest option and the one with the most certain outcome.

The boat creaked and swayed in the water, and the heavy diesel engine popped quietly somewhere at the back, near the doors to the lower deck where the other refugees were kept.

She wouldn't be missed.

Militants had been moving in even as Bella and Yana had escaped the city, and they'd heard from other refugees that people had been slaughtered like animals on the street. A young man who they had met in Turkey had told them that the thousands killed were the lucky ones; the ones who survived with no chance of escape were now living in hell.

She longed to be with her family again.

Bella timed her climb over the handrail with the gentle

sway of the boat and then stood to peer into the welcoming black arms of death.

She gave a final glance ahead, yet did not see the mountains that supposedly surrounded Athens. Behind, Turkey had become a distant memory. Below her was where she would end her journey, on her terms.

Bella leaned forward with both arms outstretched behind her, clinging to the rail. Tears rolled silently from her eyes, but she did not sob.

It was time.

She offered a small prayer to her God, to her family and to Yana, and spared them all one last thought.

Bella closed her eyes, released her grip on the handrail and waited for the deep, cool water to embrace her.

But she did not fall. She hung in the air, suspended above death. Once more, her journey had been halted by choice: heaven or hell.

Life or death.

A strong hand reached from behind. She felt herself being hoisted back over the handrail and carried in the air like a sack to the back of the boat, back to the others.

And then down.

She was unceremoniously dumped on the floor at the feet of her silent and scared companions. Then darkness engulfed her once more, as the wooden doors slammed shut.

"Where did you go?" whispered the young man that Bella had been sitting with before. "You know they will kill you for this?"

She didn't reply.

"Bella? We must play by their rules if we are to survive, and we must stick together."

"What if I do not *want* to survive?" she replied. "What if it is death that is the most inviting?"

"But Bella, think of England. It is a safe place for us. There will be opportunity."

"Is that what you believe? Do you think that our safety or opportunity lies in England? It is just another unknown. It is just another journey."

There was silence in the small cell below deck.

"But, Bella, what about the baby? Think of the baby."

"My baby stays with me, and all the time it lives and breathes inside my body, it is with me," said Bella, clutching her swollen tummy with both hands. "If I die, my baby dies with me. I will take it to a place where no harm can come to us anymore."

"Bella, you have to understand," said the young man in the darkness. "When you escape, they punish us *all*. I am sure that now we will not be given our ration of water. But when you say these things, God himself will punish you alone. Your baby may enjoy the paradise of heaven, but I am afraid that *you* will not."

As if the spoken words were heard by something far greater, the low rumble of the diesel engine stopped and Bella heard the lick and slurp of the water once more.

She wondered if she would get another chance.

Men's voices, loud but muffled, came from outside. Bella felt the boat bump against something larger than itself.

Another boat? Or was it land?

Had they arrived in Athens already?

The others remained silent, waiting for the doors to open, and for their chance at freedom to begin. Nine frightened pairs of eyes stared at her in the dim light, clinging to hope.

Bella sat in silence, waiting for death to take her by the hand.

But it wasn't the hand of death that reached in and grabbed her by the hair; it was the hand of the man with the big crooked nose and the wandering hands of the devil himself. Fernando.

She was yanked from the cell and briefly saw the stunned faces of her fellow refugees return to darkness when the door slammed shut again behind her. Up on deck, Fernando forced her to board another boat, and then stepped across to join her.

"Call me when you reach Athens," he called to two men who stood at the boat controls. He then shoved Bella down three small steps, once more into darkness.

"But Fernando, what do we tell the boss?" one of the men replied.

The man with the crooked nose closed the two small doors, leaving Bella once more with just the darkness to keep her company.

"Tell him, I have other plans for her and to be grateful it is only one I am taking," he called out.

Other plans?

Bella found a fishing net in the darkness and curled up as best she could within her new surroundings. Once the boat had started moving, she knew Fernando would not come for her. She even managed to sleep a little, a benefit of her willingness to die. With the worry of what *might be* put to one side, her dreams of what was certain provided a dark yet welcome finality.

A peace.

Time passed neither slow or fast; it just passed. But when the two little doors were eventually yanked open, and Fernando stepped down into her cabin, she knew the gates of hell had been opened.

2

MONSTER

"Morning, handsome," said Melody. "How's the weather there?"

"It's okay," replied Harvey. "It's not raining."

"It's not raining? Is that your only description of the weather?"

"What do you want me to say, Melody?" he said with a smile. "The sky's blue and the birds are singing? It's the south of France, the weather is always nice."

Melody sighed. "I guess that's about as much as I should expect from you, isn't it?"

Harvey didn't reply. He continued to lean against the doorframe looking out over their small plot of land, which Melody had begun to use for growing vegetables, and which doubled as her rifle range.

"London's nice, in case you were wondering," said Melody, pushing for conversation. "I love the fresh morning walks from the station to the office, wrapped up in a scarf and warmed by my coffee."

"Is that your way of saying it's cold?" asked Harvey. "What's the case about? What's Reg got you working on?"

"Come on, you know I can't tell you that," replied Melody. "But it does seem to be going well."

"How long do you think you'll be in London for?"

"Until we're done. Reg thinks he's on to something and we have ground units in place, so hopefully, it's a hot lead and we can wrap it up."

"Sounds interesting," said Harvey. "Another solve for your diary, eh?"

"Stop digging for clues. I can't give you any more details. I had to sign the secrets act again and all sorts of non-disclosure agreements. Anyway, what are you doing today? Will you be hitting that roof you've been meaning to fix?"

"The roof?" said Harvey.

"Don't play games with *me*, Harvey Stone. You've been telling me you'll fix that roof for a *year* now."

"I'll tell you what, Melody, you go and play at being James Bond with your mates in London, and I'll take care of things over here in the sunshine. How does that sound?"

Melody laughed. "You're so non-committal."

"Are you going to let me finish my coffee in peace?"

"Okay, enjoy yourself over there," said Melody. "I miss you, Harvey."

"Speak soon, yeah? Take care."

Harvey hit the disconnect button and placed the phone on the kitchen table. He had a habit of placing things perfectly symmetrical to their surroundings. It was a practice that he wasn't sure if he'd picked up from his foster father, who was always meticulous about such things, or his mentor, Julios, who had explained that remembering how you leave things, a room, a phone, or a pen, is an easy way to see if an intruder has been. Either way, Harvey had been able to shake off the life of crime, but never the habits that were the core of his success, and often the reason he was still alive.

Boon, Harvey's dog, sat expectantly on the tiled floor,

looking up at his master and waiting for breakfast. Harvey poured out some dry food and stood at the open door of his little farmhouse looking out at the fields beyond.

Harvey usually started his day with a run. Then he would chip away at the jobs that needed doing to the house before either heading to the beach or for a ride on his motorbike along the winding French country lanes. The house had come a long way since he'd bought it. He'd sealed the windows and painted the woodwork, but Melody was right, the roof needed doing before winter came around again.

Harvey swallowed the rcmainder of his coffee, rolled his head from left to right with two satisfying clicks of his neck, and then called to Boon. "Are you coming?"

Boon's ears pricked up, and he sprang to his feet.

"Come on then," said Harvey.

Boon's paws tapped across the tiles and he scampered through the doorway, ready for his morning run. Harvey gave the house a glance, taking a mental image. Then he pulled the door closed behind him and locked it.

His run varied from day to day. Another thing he'd learned long ago from his mentor was to try and avoid using the same route twice. Habits made it easier to catch people, a fact he'd exploited many times himself while forming plans to take down his own targets.

Harvey ran across his land and into the thick forest that stood on the boundary of the property. He hurdled fallen trees and picturesque streams then burst through an over-grown hedge into the adjacent, freshly-ploughed fields that bore the signs of early spring. The paddocks, fields and forests that surrounded his home allowed him ample opportunities to try different routes.

As easy as it was to run a new route each day, Harvey always finished at the beach near his home. He knew it was a mistake, and each day he did it, Julios' words came to life in his mind. But the beach was perfect for a final sprint, and in some weird way, by going against what Julios had told him to do so often, Harvey confirmed that his old life was over. Now he trod a new path where habits were allowed, his enemies were either dead or far away, and in the criminal world, Harvey Stone was a mere memory to the few that ever laid eyes on him and survived; a new generation of villains had emerged.

Harvey walked the last hundred yards along his private dirt driveway, a small muddy track between his own land and his neighbour's. He used the walk as his warm down, and it gave him time to stretch his legs.

Stopping halfway along the driveway, he reached down to his feet, folding himself in half and gripping his toes between fingers and thumbs. Then he worked his head lower, stretching his back and glutes until, by holding the back of his legs, he could place his forehead against his knees.

That was when he saw the fresh tyre tracks in the mud.

They were of an SUV or bigger, judging by the width. Melody drove a little sports car and she'd been gone a few days already. Harvey's bike had hybrid tyres.

Someone else had driven along the drive.

Harvey's senses pricked. He took a quick look around. He hadn't seen any cars on the return from his run. It was early morning for the sleepy, coastal village; the tourists would come later. Harvey wasn't expecting anybody. Visitors were rare.

He checked the house. The front door was shut and bolted from the inside as it always was. The windows looked intact, locked and exactly how he'd left them. Nothing seemed out of place.

Except for the tyre tracks.

He moved to the rear of the house, taking a wide arc and surveying his land. It was seemingly devoid of life.

It was when he reached the back door and found the envelope pinned to the wood that he knew trouble had come knocking.

———

"How's the progress going?" said Jackson, as he stepped into the operations room.

"Radio silence, sir," replied Reg. "We have Gibson and Sharp in the country, but so far, neither has made contact."

"So what's the protocol?"

"They have trackers, sir, so we can see where they are."

"But you can't talk to them?"

"Not as yet. We're trying but have had no response. They have comms kits, but right now, it's unknown if these are being blocked by the Greek authorities."

"And do we have any idea of who is running the show yet?"

"Not yet, sir. That's why the two operatives were sent. They were both briefed and told not to engage. We're expecting a report back in two hours' time. If we don't hear anything, we'll send in some backup."

"Okay," said Jackson. "Nothing heavy. This is a straight-forward investigation. I had hoped we'd have straightforward answers by now."

Jackson stepped out of the operations room and closed the door behind him.

"He's on your case," said Ladyluck from the far end of a central row of tables.

"Thanks, Ladyluck, I'll deal with Jackson. You just find me Gibson and Sharp," said Reg.

He turned back to his screen and ran another ping test on the two men's comms kit.

"I know that look," said Melody. "You're worried about them."

"Of course I'm worried, Melody. I sent three men to Athens to carry out some surveillance, one of whom has been missing for a week, the other two we haven't heard from for eight hours."

"But we can see them on screen," said Jess. "That's something, isn't it?"

"I think we all know that doesn't mean they're alive," said Reg. "How many times have we chased after Harvey only to find a pile of clothes in a field?"

"Oh, come on, we can't compare these two guys to Harvey. These are trained men. They know the protocols. They know the moves."

Reg shoved his keyboard away and sat back.

"Reg, take it easy," said Jess.

"Yeah, I'm sure they'll be fine."

"I just don't want to have to make those calls, Melody," he whispered. "To their wives, you know? We already lost Harper. We can't afford to lose another."

"Harper knew the risks, Reg," said Jess. "He was the first man in, and instead of doing what he was told, he went off-piste and landed himself in hot water. If he'd just done what he was told in the first place, first of all, he'd still be alive, and secondly, they wouldn't know we're on to them. We'd have eyes on the ground feeding us information so we can intercept the delivery. How much simpler could it get?"

"But he didn't, Jess, did he?" argued Reg. "No. He used his own judgment without our support, got caught and now anyone I send out there is in danger from the moment the wheels hit the ground."

Jess turned away, clearly displeased with Reg's reaction. She was the baby of the team. Her last name, Jones, was never used.

When an operative went to Jess with a problem to be researched, they didn't address a cold last name. Instead, they sat with a Jess, a real person who understood what they were trying to achieve. Everyone knew Jess well enough to use her first name. She'd helped them all at some point. Although she and Reg had been an item for over a year, work was work, and she sucked up Reg's snappy comment with professional distaste.

"So send more men," said Melody.

"Excuse me?" said Reg. "Did you just hear what we said?"

"I heard," said Melody. "Send two operatives to track down Gibson and Sharp. Who are the two new guys?"

Reg glanced at the far end of the room.

"You mean Derby and Barnet?"

"Yeah, send them. Let them prove themselves," said Melody.

"It might come to that," replied Reg. "I don't like it though."

"Where'd they transfer from anyway?" asked Melody. "They look like they know what they're doing."

"Can't really say, Melody," said Reg. He turned his head to face her. "Even if I knew."

"They don't tell you? Don't you get their career history?"

"I just run the operations, Melody."

"So?"

"So what?"

"Are you going to send them?"

"I know you're right, but let's hang on," said Reg. "I don't want to jump to conclusions until we know Gibson and Sharp are definitely in some kind of trouble."

"By the time Gibson and Sharp are found, it'll be too late. We've already lost our eyes on the ground."

Reg leaned back in his chair and gave a loud exhale of frustrated air.

"Derby," he called to the other side of the room.

"Sir?"

"Get yourself set up," said Reg. "You and Barnet are going to Athens."

———

"What do you mean they got in your way?" Fernando shouted into the phone. "You're a smart guy, aren't you? Or do I need to find someone smarter?"

Bella tried her hardest to hear the voice on the other end of the phone, but Fernando had moved away and was pacing the boat.

"Undercover agents? So take care of them. We have a boatful arriving in Athens in approximately thirty minutes. Make sure they reach the lorry or-"

Fernando's voice lowered to almost a growl.

"Listen to me, Streaky, if the agents stand in your way, get rid of them like the last one. We need to get these people through, or the boss will have us all dumped in the sea, and hey, *I* am not going to be the one to take the rap. Take care of it." Fernando paused. "What do you mean where am *I*? Don't you worry so much about what I'm doing. You just concentrate on getting rid of those agents, and getting those trucks ready."

From where Bella lay below deck, Fernando seemed to be getting angrier and angrier. She couldn't face any more of the man's temper. He was like a coiled spring.

"I don't care what Jimmy told you, Streaky." Fernando's voice had risen again to an excited yell. "I took *one* as a guarantee, and I'm keeping her safe. There's nine more in Jimmy's boat. Lock them in the workshop and see to it that they make the truck tomorrow."

He disconnected the call.

Bella heard Fernando walking above her. He was confident on the boat, walking naturally with the movements of the waves as if he'd been at sea for many years. She also noticed that this new boat rocked much less than the other one. Maybe Fernando was more skilled than the previous captain.

She lay in darkness on the scratchy, smelly fishing nets, listening to his footsteps. Her body tensed each time it sounded like he was close by, near the back of the boat.

She was dreading the doors opening again.

Bella wondered what would happen. Her English wasn't perfect, but it was good enough to understand the one-sided conversation Fernando had spoken with somebody called Streaky. The others were going to be loaded onto another truck. That had been the plan for her; that was what she had paid for. The last leg of her journey.

Would she be going too? Would she be reunited with them eventually? Or had *her* path now changed?

She would choose her own path when the time was right.

"Boss?" she heard Fernando say. He was using the telephone again, but this time his tone was different, more submissive.

"No, I've told him to take care of it. The boat should be arriving any time now."

Fernando paced above her once more. He took long, slow steps instead of the shorter more agitated ones he had taken before.

"Yes, I have taken one for security," said Fernando. "No, boss, she is *not* for my own pleasure. This one is a troublemaker."

The pacing stopped. Bella listened intently to the one-sided conversation.

"Yes, it's a girl."

"What do you mean is she pretty? What do you think I-?"

"No, boss. I'll keep her on my boat. I have an idea."

"Yes, boss."

"I know. They will send more men and they will just keep coming."

"I don't know how they found us. In fact, as I remember, it was your job to see that our operation remained invisible, but now I see even you aren't able to stop their meddling. We'll need to find alternatives in the future. Athens is no longer safe for us. But most of all, it is important that we encourage Harvey Stone to join us here. We will kill two birds with one stone. Or should I say all the birds and the Stone."

"Oh, he will come. It's what he does. In fact, I have already reached out to him. But I think maybe he will need some gentle persuasion."

"No, boss. I asked him to join us a few months ago. But he's retired now, so he'll need convincing. I'm sure I have the means."

"I'm so sure because his moral compass is his weakness. Give me one of the refugees and I'll have him for sure."

"Yes, boss, I know I already *hurt* them. But clearly, he needs further encouragement. I think perhaps one of the younger ones. It will be a small sacrifice to pay for such a grand finale to Mr Stone's life."

Fernando disconnected the call, sighed out loud, and took four slow, deliberate steps towards the back of the boat.

No harm will come to her. That's what he'd said.

Bella clung to that thought as the two small wooden doors opened. Fernando stooped low and peered inside. He stood silhouetted by the dawn sun. Bella couldn't make out his features or his expression but saw that he was removing his belt. She huddled herself against the wall and tucked her bare feet into the dirty nets.

"What do you want?" she cried.

"Bella, Bella, Bella," he said with a mock soothing voice.

"Leave me alone," she said. "Please. Just don't touch me."

Fernando stood over her with his belt in his hand, rocking the leather strap back and forth. His other hand was slowly unfastening the buttons on his trousers.

"We can do this the hard way, Bella," he said. "Or we can do this the even harder way."

3

CARROT ON A STICK

"Sir, you might want to see this," said Jess, leaning back as she moved her computer's video output to one of the large wall-mounted screens above them.

"Who's that?" asked Reg. He tracked the little red icon that moved across the satellite imagery screen.

"Gibson, sir."

"He's in a boat?" asked Reg, a little surprised.

"Looks like it. He still hasn't checked in though."

"And Sharp?" asked Reg. "Any news from him?"

"Not a dicky bird, sir."

"Do we have him on screen at least?"

"Nope. He disappeared last night," replied Jess. "He was by the boatyard for a while, but then just vanished while we were in the meeting."

"Vanished?"

"Vanished, sir," said Jess. "Could be two reasons-"

"He's underground-"

"Or he's underwater," finished Jess.

"Or he's just plain old had everything stripped off him and dumped in the sea," offered Melody. "It wouldn't be the first time that had happened, would it?" Melody raised an eyebrow to Reg. She was referring to an incident where Harvey had his clothes stripped off his body, leaving the team clueless about his whereabouts.

Reg fell silent and stared at the red dot on the screen as it moved slowly out to deeper water, away from the mainland into the Mediterranean.

"I know where I'd put my money," said Ladyluck under her breath.

Reg span around and immediately realised that the whole office had been watching the screen too. One of their colleagues, who had been missing for two days, was very possibly being led out to sea to be dumped in the ocean, and another one was missing.

"Keep your thoughts to yourself please, Ladyluck," muttered Reg.

"Jess, can we try to get hold of him?" asked Reg. "Just keep trying."

"I've had an open call out to the pair of them for nearly forty-eight hours now, sir," replied Jess. "Sat phones are off and the comms aren't being responded to. We ran some network tests and the devices are responding, so they're operational, but neither of the men are responding."

"Can we get a live satellite feed on that boat please, someone?"

Jess's fingers sprang into life. Within a few moments, the large wall-mounted screen beside the satellite tracker displayed an aerial view of the world. Then the image zoomed closer and closer until the continents became countries, and countries became cities, until finally Athens and the Mediterranean filled the screen. The image zoomed in at the satellite camera's maximum range and the city was pushed off screen. A pixelated image of a tiny boat surrounded by the ocean remained on the screen.

"Is that the best we can do?" asked Reg.

"That's the only satellite we can access in the region right now, sir," said Jess, "without drawing attention to the operation."

"I feel so helpless," said the woman beside Ladyluck. "I mean, can't we call the Greek authorities or something?"

"And tell them what?" asked Reg. "That we're sorry but we seem to have misplaced two of our secret service agents in your lovely city, and we think another might be about to-"

"Don't say it," said Jess.

"It doesn't need saying anyway," said Reg.

The boat had stopped. The satellite image grew a little clearer, but was still not clear enough for the team to identify individual people. It was just a blurred picture of two men struggling with something heavy. Within a few moments, there was no need to watch.

The red dot on the overhead screen blinked off and a tiny beeping alarm started on Jess' central computer. The entire team stared at the two screens in silent disbelief.

"Switch that off," said Reg. He lowered his head. "Let's all take a moment, team, to remember Gibson and spare a thought for his family."

Reg stood giddy on his feet while around him his team dealt with the blow in their own ways. Some of them closed their eyes. Some looked at the floor. Manners, who sat beside Ladyluck, mouthed a silent prayer to herself.

"Thank you, everyone," said Reg. "Jess, follow that boat. We need the identification mark. There must be a port authority number on it. Ladyluck, start making arrangements."

"Arrangements, sir?" Ladyluck replied. "What for?"

"We're relocating the operations team," said Reg. "We're not going to catch this lot sat here. We're *all* going to Athens."

―――――

Harvey took a slow climb down the ladder with a pile of broken roof tiles on his shoulder and dumped them in a rubbish skip. He'd been slowly filling it over the past few months. Behind his garage was a stack of new tiles that he'd bought. It wasn't many, but enough to replace the broken ones dotted around the roof. Winter would arrive before he knew it. Anyway, where better a place to keep an eye on his property than on the roof? The note had jarred Harvey. The work took his mind off the note, but his senses had been pricked.

He collected two of the new tiles, walked back to the ladder and began the long climb up. Slotting them in was easy on the lower rows. He'd just hooked the lowest tile over the roof baton when he caught sight of a black SUV travelling very slowly along the lane towards the beach. It was nothing; cars used the lane all the time. But Harvey noted the make and model and eyed it as it drove past.

The driver stared back at him.

It took another two hours to replace the broken tiles. The sun was rising high, the day heading into peak tourist time. More cars began to venture along the lane, but not the black SUV.

The beach was just two minutes away. Although the town of Argylles did not see as many tourists as places like Marseille or Montpellier, which were both a few hours along the coast, many people who hunted for the quieter coastal spots eventually found the place Harvey called home. The cars became frequent as the morning grew later, but he kept his eye on the traffic. An old habit.

Soon after Harvey had finished the roof, he stood in his kitchen at the back door with a coffee in his hand. Boon was sleeping somewhere inside the house.

The photo on the kitchen counter drew his attention once more.

Why would someone want him?

The photograph felt sticky as if it had been recently printed. It showed a young girl in a small, poorly lit room. Her hands and feet were tied, her nose was bloodied, and her eye swollen. She had clearly been beaten. It wasn't the most shocking thing Harvey had seen. In fact, he'd done far worse to people himself. But what did the photo mean?

He tried to recall the face, but it was nobody he knew or remembered, and he thought himself to be pretty good at remembering faces. Scribbled on the back had been a small cryptic message. *You can stop this. FF.*

The message was correct; Harvey probably could stop whatever was happening. But why would he get involved in what looked like it could be a lot of trouble? Someone else's trouble. He'd had enough of his own adventures. He didn't need to go and fight someone else's battles.

But who was it? And how did they know where he lived?

The note had been signed *FF*.

The fields behind his little farmhouse were perfect for thinking, just wide, open fields that stretched on forever, dotted with small forests. The scene allowed the mind to wander where it wanted, almost as if it was itself walking in the fields.

Maybe someone had gotten his name from somebody else. Someone fighting for beaten housewives, perhaps? Maybe the photo was just generic or staged as a trap. But he knew it wasn't. Harvey had seen enough to know that it was a real photo with a real girl in a real room.

With real blood on her dirtied face.

Harvey picked up the image up for the twentieth time. "She's foreign," he said aloud. "The clothes, the skin, the headscarf."

He studied the photo further.

"That's a fishing net that she's lying on."

Harvey held the photo into the light.

"The walls are wood and the..." Harvey stopped. He pictured the scene. It was suddenly clear in his mind.

It was a boat. The girl was on a boat.

Was it in France? Was it close by? Was that why someone had asked him to help?

Footsteps crunched on the loose stones to the side of the house. Harvey pushed the back door closed and stepped into the shadows. The footsteps grew closer and slowed; whoever it was knew to be quiet.

An arm reached out, ready to pin another photo to his door. Harvey wrenched the door open and grabbed the wrist tight.

"Non, non. S'il vous plaît. Ne me blessé pas," cried the young French boy, his eyes wide with fear.

Harvey dragged him inside and continued to grip his arm. He snatched the photo from him. "Where is this?" he asked.

The boy just shook his head.

"Où?" shouted Harvey.

The boy instinctively glanced towards the lane and held up a five-euro note. Harvey pulled him through the house to the bedroom where the windows looked out onto the long drive and the lane beyond. He pulled the edge of the curtain back. A glimmer of light reflected off a car window parked in full view at the end of his drive. Before Harvey could react, the car pulled off abruptly.

It was the black SUV he'd seen earlier. Harvey recalled one man driving alone, no kids, and he hadn't seen any baggage.

"Go," he said to the kid. He released his grip and pointed to the door but remained staring at the new photo.

The boy ran back through the house, past Boon, who had

woken and ventured out from the couch to see what was happening, and out into the field. The door crashed closed behind him.

Harvey watched through the window as the boy ran the length of his driveway without looking back then turned right, heading inland towards the village.

The photo was a similar scene, but with a different girl.

He turned away in disgust. It was clear that she'd been more than just beaten.

Harvey sat the new photo beside the old one in the kitchen then flipped it over face down.

The party has started. Your presence is required. FF.

———

"So you expect him to make contact soon, do you?" said Fernando.

Bella was amazed that the pig could take a phone call so calmly after what he'd just done to her. She wiped her eyes with the back of her hand and pulled her dress down to cover herself, thankful for the darkness of the cabin. She couldn't bear to look at the damage he'd caused.

Bella had been horrified when he'd used his phone to take a photo while he hurt her. She'd hidden her face with her hands, but he'd just pulled them away and told her to smile. Then, he'd seemed proud when he sent the photo to somebody.

Am I being sold?

She dry heaved at the thought of him inside her. Never would she forget that sickening sensation. His odour, his breath and his crooked nose would always haunt her. Bella had worked herself up. Her breathing had quickened, and her dry throat rasped. But not for long.

"We need him here in Athens, Rascal. Don't let him run

away with the idea that hurting you is going to achieve anything," said Fernando. "I've seen him in action. The man's a beast, and if you're not careful, he'll take you down before you even know he's there. Stay local, stay visible, and get him on your side. I'll take care of him when he's here."

Even from outside on the deck, Fernando's voice nauseated Bella. There was no going forward for her now. A few hours ago, she'd had a choice: life or death. Now all she had was the hope that Fernando got her to England where she may be able to put the terrible journey behind her and start afresh, somehow.

But even if he did...

Bella knew she wouldn't be able to live with herself now. She was dirty. Her timing needed to be right. It would need to be soon before they arrived on land.

I'm carrying the child of the devil, she thought.

Bella pushed herself up onto her knees and winced at the pain he'd caused, sharp like daggers below her dress. Something had torn and she'd bled.

She tried the doors but they didn't budge. She peered through the crack between them and saw that Fernando had pushed something through the handles to stop them from opening, a piece of wood maybe. Bella fell back onto the nets and curled up into a ball.

"Keep me posted, Rascal," said Fernando, his phone call coming to an end. "If he doesn't reach out today, I'll send another photo, and this time, he'll respond for sure."

Bella's heart sank. She would need to find a way to die before then. But in the darkness and with the doors locked, she would have no chance. If Fernando needed another photo, worse than before, then perhaps an opportunity would arise.

She would take the devil child with her.

What he'd done to her had been excruciating, but it was

the ease at which he'd done it that had seemed to make it worse. The man had no remorse. He was pure evil. His footsteps on the deck above acted as a reminder that the devil walked close by.

Bella thought back to happier times, desperate to push the bitter taste of him out of her mouth. Her body. Her mind.

She thought of her mother. She remembered how they would sit and talk for hours about all the things that had been and all that might be. Her mother had warned Bella that she would need to find the right man, a kind man, to enjoy her life with. Some men, her mother had warned, would take everything and give nothing back. But the right man would wait until it was offered and when the time was right; that would be the man to bare her children for.

Fernando had taken what he'd wanted with ease.

Had he done it before?

He would do it again, for sure. Maybe Bella could finish them both, herself and Fernando. Her own life might be over, but maybe she could help and save the lives of others. Perhaps she could sink the boat. Perhaps the deed would work in her favour as she stood on the cusp of heaven and hell, a tainted woman carrying the devil's child, unworthy of heaven's grace.

The boat's engine started up again. She hadn't even noticed it had stopped, but thinking back, it had fallen silent just before he'd opened the door. At least he wouldn't touch her while the boat was moving.

She moved again to the two doors and peered through the tiny crack. It was daylight still, and the blue sea and sky seemed to merge.

Bella had seen the small canopy above the wheel. It had been about halfway along the boat. If Fernando was steering, would he hear if she broke out?

She pushed gently on one side of the doors.

It didn't move.

She pushed a little harder.

The corner gave a little.

Harder still.

She could feel the cool air on her hands.

Bella grasped the other door and applied pressure. She found that it flexed more than the first.

Hope peered tentatively from the darkness.

The door seemed to be made of long wooden panels. If she could just break one free, maybe she could get an arm out then remove whatever Fernando had wedged between the handles.

Her heart pounded. If he caught her, who knew what else he was capable of doing.

Bella laid on her back and put the heel of her right foot against the first wooden panel. She raised her arms above her head and held onto the wooden wall.

She pushed.

The door flexed but remained.

Deep breaths and hope filled her thoughts. She would have limited time if she managed to break through.

On a count of three, she told herself. Her breathing began to quicken.

Strength.

Three.

Freedom.

Two.

Mother.

4

THE BEAST AWAKENS

"RIGHT TEAM, LET'S GET OURSELVES READY," SAID REG, AS the private jet taxied along the airfield towards the awaiting cars.

"We'll take the van, sir," said Derby. "Barnet and me."

"Good," said Reg. "That leaves four of us. Jess, Melody, Ladyluck, you ride with me in the car. I want to get to the safe house and get surveillance set up, and I want to be set up by nightfall."

"What do we have for a safe house?" asked Melody, looking around at the team. "A villa?"

"It's a two-bed apartment opposite the boatyard, maybe thirty to forty minutes' drive from here," said Ladyluck. She was pleased with her ability to organise the plane, the safe house and transport in under two hours.

"And presumably we're not going to blaze through Athens in an unmarked black BMW?" replied Melody, donning her sunglasses and letting her hair fall over her tight leather jacket.

"There's a financial crisis, Mills," said Ladyluck, reaching for her small case from the overhead. "Arriving in the industrial area in a BMW would be like painting targets on our backs."

Melody ducked down and peered through the window. An old car and a beat-up van were parked beside each other at the furthest end of the private runway. They stood away from the buildings and sheltered by stationary planes.

"They look like they won't even make the forty minute journey," said Melody.

"So they're the perfect disguise. They'll fit right in." Ladyluck smiled as she sat back down in her seat. "Passports out everyone. We'll be greeted by officials and then left to our own devices. He's friendly, but if he tests you, we're on a business trip."

"A business trip?" said Derby, from the seat behind her. "We have a flight case full of automatic weapons, and enough rounds to start world war three."

"This is Greece, Derby. If you want me to put it into perspective, *you* have more money than Greece in your savings account," replied Ladyluck in her best authoritative tone and clearly loving being the centre of attention. "You'll be surprised at the questions they don't ask when you cross their palms with silver."

Derby laughed. "Yeah and paper notes with the Queen's head on."

"You can be sure of that." Ladyluck smiled and gave him a wink.

"We'll load the van," said Derby. "You guys go ahead and get the place secure. We'll follow up with the gear."

Reg nodded his appreciation.

The private jet jerked to a stop, and Ladyluck stood again to be the first to exit.

At the bottom of the stairs stood two men, one in an ill-fitting cheap suit and one in a fine, light suit with a brown leather belt and shoes. A pair of sunglasses finished his polished look. Behind them were two cars and the old van. One of the cars was a nearly new silver Audi; the other was an old black Peugeot. Melody could easily guess which vehicle belonged to which man, and which one was the official taking backhanders from the British government.

Melody stood third in the queue to disembark and then stepped out into the beautiful Greek sunshine. The feeling of warmth on her face was a pleasant change from the bitter London wind. It lifted her spirits immediately. The man with the shades and fine suit inspected their passports. He waved them on without so much as a hi or goodbye, unashamedly holding the brown envelope that Ladyluck had passed him under his arm as he did.

Melody had been missing Harvey. It was always the same while she was away. She wasn't full time with Reg's team and hadn't taken on too many jobs for him, but when she did, she missed home. She missed Boon and the house. The Greece operation had escalated from a simple human trafficking case to something far more sinister, and when agents had begun to disappear, Reg had asked for her help.

Maybe when it was over, she could stay out there for a while, she thought, and ask Harvey to join her for a holiday. As long as the plan went smoothly, they'd all be out in a few days. Some quality time with Harvey in Greece might be just what the doctor ordered.

It was Melody's first time in Athens. She sat silently looking out of the car window during the ride from the airfield, noting the simple houses and visible poverty. Despite Greece's ongoing financial situation, the forest-covered hills and glorious sunshine conveyed a sense of peace. It was a reminder that money wasn't the answer to everyone's happiness.

They crested a hill and looked down over the sprawling city of Athens. From above, it seemed to fill every space the valley floor had to offer, from the mountains that surrounded it to the beautiful blue sea below. Generic low-rise buildings stood side by side in pastel whites, blues and yellows, while the older, grander and often ancient buildings commanded the open space around them. In the centre of the city, atop the tallest rocky outcrop, stood the remains of an ancient citadel and landmark: the Acropolis.

The drive through the vibrant city gave a clear picture of life in Athens. Small squares hidden in backstreets teemed with life, where coffee shops and boutique clothes stores were hives of activity. Narrow streets with graffiti-covered buildings fed like river tributaries into larger roads with open squares, often featuring a central statue or monument. Melody recognised international chains and high-end designer stores in small pockets of affluence. Other areas housed tiny shops and street stalls, crammed with second-hand furniture, paintings, clocks, and anything that might raise a few euros.

The apartment that Ladyluck had organised was on the south side of the city at the north end of the coastline. There seemed to be much less traffic on the roads, fewer people on the streets and less wealth invested into the poorly maintained buildings.

"Mobile two, this is mobile one. Come back," said Reg into his radio.

"Mobile two," said Derby from the van.

"Mobile two, what's your ETA?" asked Reg.

"We're loaded and just coming down into Athens now. About thirty minutes behind you."

"Good," said Reg. "Mobile two, go find some coffee and maybe pick up water and supplies. We'll go in and set up surveillance. We don't want six people seen carrying boxes and bags into the apartment, so we'll arrive in batches."

"Copy," came the reply.

"Melody, can you check the roof? We need eyes all around, and that'll be your perch with the sniper rifle," said Reg, as he flicked through some photos of the boatyard in his folder.

"Yep," said Melody, snapping out of her daydream.

"Are you okay, Melody?" asked Ladyluck. "You seem quiet."

"Yeah, just missing home, I guess," replied Melody without turning away from the window.

"I'm sure this will be over in a few days, Melody," said Reg.

The driver stopped the car outside a rundown apartment block facing a row of boatyards. The area bordered an industrial part of town. Chain link fences opposite the building acted as a perimeter for the boatyards.

"Is that our boatyard?" asked Melody.

"Yes, the middle one," replied Ladyluck.

"Security is pretty dire. Shouldn't be too hard to get inside."

"We need to see what they're doing before we send any more agents in, Melody. I can't risk anyone else."

"Copy that," replied Melody.

She scanned the grounds of the boatyard. Vast, open areas were dotted with scrapped or decrepit boats on trailers. Engines and loose parts lay scattered in the spaces between the trailers, and wild dogs patrolled the area in their perpetual hunt for food.

Melody peered up at the apartment building. It looked completely empty. "Looks nice, Ladyluck," she said. "Who's your travel agent?"

"It might not be a five-star hotel, Melody," replied Ladyluck. "But it's facing the boatyard, and I think you'll find it has all the amenities we need."

"I'm sure it's fine," said Reg, as he pushed his door open

and climbed out of the car. "Two at a time. Jess, you're with me. Melody, Ladyluck, wait for my signal then follow."

Melody observed as Reg held the door open for Jess then followed her inside. Ladyluck caught Melody watching them.

"Cute, aren't they?" she said.

"She's nice," said Melody. "He deserves someone like her."

"He tells me you used to work together, full time, I mean."

"Yeah, we've spent the best part of ten years on various teams. Reg is a solid guy."

"And what do you think about him *running* this team?" asked Ladyluck. "You think he can handle it? I mean, he was just a researcher, a tech guy."

"Reg has seen more action than he lets on," replied Melody. "And he's capable of a lot more than you think. Are you having trouble with him?"

"No," said Ladyluck. "But I do doubt his ability to handle the decision making. It's a tough job."

"Do you?" replied Melody. "On what grounds?"

Ladyluck knew she'd overstepped the mark. "Well, he's not-"

"You don't know what he is or what he isn't," snapped Melody. "And all I've seen from you so far is negativity and pessimism. So why don't you keep your opinions to yourself? Give Reg a chance and, who knows, you might even learn something from him."

"Well, I-"

"Conversation's over, Ladyluck. Move on."

Melody pushed the car door open and climbed out with her rucksack.

"Hey," called Ladyluck, as she climbed out of her side. "He said to wait, right?"

"I'm done with waiting."

Melody pushed open the door to the old apartment

building and stepped inside the fresh but very basic granite-clad foyer. A single, narrow set of stairs led off to her left and a small lift door stood in front. No concierge waited to take their bags. No plants were dotted around to cheer the place up. Just cheap decor, yellowing paint and the lift door. Any sign of previous tenants lay beneath a thick layer of dust.

The door opened behind her and Ladyluck stepped inside. Melody turned to glance her way, but Ladyluck averted her eyes.

"It's the top floor," said Ladyluck, hinting at the small lift.

Melody hit the button and a single door squeaked to one side, revealing a space ample enough for two people, but no more.

"Cosy," said Ladyluck.

Melody didn't reply. She stepped in and hit the button for the top floor. The doors struggled but eventually closed. The elevator's mechanism groaned into life and slowly began to rise.

It was nearly a full minute later when the ride stopped. There were two apartments in front of them, two doors and a strong, unpleasant odour of cat urine. To Melody's immediate right was the narrow staircase leading down to the foyer. An even smaller set of stairs led up to the roof.

"They're both ours," said Ladyluck, as she stepped out behind her. "One is for sleeping, one is for working."

Melody pushed the door of the right-hand apartment, and it swung open.

"Oh jeez, is that-?"

"Cat piss," said Melody. "I'm guessing we'll be sleeping in the other one."

She nudged the left-hand door and let it swing back to hit the wall.

"Reg?" she called.

There was no reply.

Melody stepped inside the apartment. There was a small kitchen to the right with a bathroom beside it, and then three larger rooms off the small corridor. Bright light spilt through the large west-facing windows into the lounge.

Melody stepped into the hallway.

"Reg? Jess?" she called, louder than before.

"Maybe they're on the roof?" asked Ladyluck.

Melody reached for her radio. "Tenant, come back."

No reply.

"Say that again?" said Ladyluck, cocking her head to one side.

Melody gave the call again over the radio.

"Sounds like it's coming from in here," said Ladyluck, opening the door to one of the bedrooms. "It is. Look, it's his radio. He must have dropped it."

"Reg wouldn't drop that," said Melody with urgency. "Check the other apartment. I'll check the roof."

Melody ran to the stairs. She hadn't even reached the roof when the entire top floor filled with Ladyluck's chilling scream.

———

There weren't many places to hide in the village of Argylles. Finding a rental car was easy for Harvey, as he rode his motorbike along the little high street. There were no hotels, just two bed and breakfasts and a few campsites.

Harvey found the SUV in under thirty minutes and found the owner less than five minutes afterwards. He was a short man. Either he was wearing a bad attempt at blending in as a tourist, in his khaki shorts and sleeveless top, or he was simply happy to be in the sunshine, where he could show off his toned arms.

To Harvey, he stood out a mile.

Harvey watched him from a distance as he emerged from one of the village's two little cafes. He was typing a message into his phone. Then he lit a cigarette and took the short walk to his car.

Harvey sized him up and began to formulate a plan. He didn't have time or energy to waste on these people. They'd somehow found him, but Harvey was sure they would leave him alone once they had heard what he had to say.

And did what he had to do.

The black SUV pulled away from the curb and took the road out of the village towards the beach, a long and winding stretch of tarmac that hugged the coast for miles. Harvey waited a full minute, and then followed.

As predicted, the man stopped the car a few miles further out of the village in front of a small cliffside bed and breakfast. Harvey assumed that staying in the centre would have been too close to Harvey's house, and any lodging further away would be inconvenient to deliver the messages. The next village was some way down the road, and even quieter than Argylles with even fewer bed and breakfasts.

The driver's door opened as Harvey approached. Harvey slid his visor up on his helmet, and came to a stop in front of the SUV to stop him from driving away. But Harvey's arrival was apparently part of the man's plan.

"I was wondering when you'd show your face," he said, smiling, as though Harvey had finally succumbed to the offers on the back of the two sick photos.

Harvey stepped off the bike, turned the engine off, and turned to face him. "What's with the pictures?"

"They say a picture says a thousand words, Mr Stone," he replied.

Harvey put the accent at European, but couldn't pinpoint the origin. He didn't reply.

"We need your help, Mr Stone. We have some people we need you to take care of."

"What makes you think that I'm looking for work? And why can't you sort them out yourself?" said Harvey. "I don't know you, I don't need money, and I certainly don't appreciate you sending little boys to my house to do your dirty work."

"Ah, the boy."

"Yeah, the boy. What are you, *nuts*? What do you think he's going to do now? He's going to tell his dad that some bloke in a black car gave him money to-"

"He won't tell anyone. I made sure of that."

Harvey didn't reply.

"So?" asked the man.

"So what?"

"Are you coming with me, or will you stay? I can assure you, the photos will only get worse." He lit another cigarette and breathed the smoke out in a long silver plume that carried in the wind. "Only you can stop the suffering, Mr Stone."

"Who do you work for?" asked Harvey. "Who's FF?"

"Ah, come on now."

"Do you know who I am?" Harvey asked.

"Well, my boss tells me great things."

"You've got the time it takes for me to count to ten before that becomes your last cigarette. Who do you work for?"

"Mr Stone-"

"Ten." Harvey took a step closer.

"You don't have a gun. You're just-"

"Nine."

Another step.

"If you hurt me, more will die."

"I don't care about anyone else," said Harvey. "Eight."

"Not even little girls?" said the man, stepping backwards. "I'm told you have morals."

"Seven."

Harvey matched his steps to maintain the distance.

"Don't you want to stop them being raped, Mr Stone?" said the man. "I can't believe you would just let them suffer."

"Six."

The man glanced backwards at where he was going and saw the cliff edge growing closer. He had nowhere to run.

"Five," said Harvey. "What do you need me to do?"

The man stopped walking backwards and held his hands up as if to stop the drama.

"Okay, okay. We have an operation. It was going well," he began. "But as you know, these things don't last. There are men, they make it hard for us, they stop our lorries."

"Four."

"We go here, they follow. We go there, they go there. They stopped our trucks. It costs money." The man's voice was becoming panicked.

"Three. Who are these people?"

"We don't know. Maybe competition? But they have to go, and my boss says good things about you."

"And who is your boss?"

The man inhaled, and his large chest rose with the air.

"Two."

"Fernando," he said finally. "Fernando Ferez."

A memory hit Harvey, and he immediately understood.

"He told me that he spoke to you a few months ago, here on the beach. He offered you work," said the man.

"And I told him I don't want work."

"Well, he-"

"What's the job?"

"I can't say, Mr Stone." The man looked apologetic. "We have to keep things tight, you know."

Harvey didn't reply.

"So you'll do it?" said the man. A wry smile crept onto his face. "You'll come to Athens with me?"

"I didn't say that," replied Harvey. "But now I know where it is and who it is for."

Harvey rolled his neck left and right.

"What? *What?*" The man glanced behind him at the cliff edge. "You won't kill me."

"Wouldn't I?"

"No. No, you won't. You want to stop the girls from being hurt, and only I can take you." He gave Harvey a smug look, lowered his hands and straightened his vest top. "So how should we do this?"

"Like this," said Harvey. He took a step forward.

The man stepped back in defence into thin air.

"One."

―――――

"One."

Bella spoke the final count aloud then slammed the heel of her foot into one of the wooden panels, which splintered and broke away from the frame. But the gap was too small for her to climb through.

She tried again on the next panel along. It took two more attempts, but eventually, she broke through.

Bella stretched through with her arm. The gap still wasn't wide enough for her body, but she could reach the chunk of wood that Fernando had wedged between the handles. She tugged on it and hit it until it clattered to the deck.

Sunlight and air washed over her, and the wake of the boat spread out before her like a winding road to the horizon. As fast as she could, she pulled herself from the cabin.

Holding onto the handrail, she took a final glance back to check Fernando hadn't seen her.

Suddenly, the engine stopped.

Fernando was nowhere to be seen. The raised cabin blocked her view of the rest of the boat. She checked the narrow gangways that ran along each side.

He must be at the front.

Seizing her chance, Bella took a tentative and painful step over the handrail with one leg. She then paused to check behind her.

Fernando's eyes locked onto hers as a lion might peer from long grass. He swung a long gaff in a wild arc. Bella couldn't move. She was stuck; her dress was caught on the old handrail. The long wooden pole caught her square in the back, knocking the wind out of her. She tried to free herself and pull her leg back, but Fernando swung the long pole once more. Bella felt the sharp hooked end of the gaff rush past just inches from her face.

Bella toppled and fell to the floor.

"You little bitch," said Fernando, seeing the damage she had done to his boat. "You're nothing but an ungrateful whore." He kicked out at her and connected with her lower back.

Bella rolled into a ball then saw her chance. If she could just stand up, she could make the leap over the side rail.

"Come here, you little-"

Bella sprang to her bare feet, took one step, placed her hands onto the stainless steel tubing, and leapt into the air. Then, with a sudden jerk to her throat, she was yanked backwards by the neck. Fernando's gaff held tight around her throat. She hit the hard deck flat on her back in a confused state of shock and pain. She writhed as her body sought to understand.

Fernando stepped across and stood over her. His nose

seemed to be even larger and more crooked from where she lay, looking up at him.

"You're beginning to be more trouble than you're worth," he said. "It's a shame."

Bella didn't reply. Her chance had gone. He would surely make her suffer now.

"Why do you want to die?" he asked. His voice softened. "You spent so long running from your home to get to England and look." He pointed to the land on the horizon. "It's not far now, maybe two days once we hit land. So why do you do these things?"

"There's nothing left for me now," she whispered. The fight inside her had dissipated, and she prepared herself for pain.

"There are many things left for you if you want them bad enough." Fernando lowered himself to a crouch beside her. "You're pretty," he said. "You just need a chance, a helping hand."

"And who is going to give me a helping hand now?" Bella replied, cradling her stomach.

Fernando dropped his eyes to her belly.

"I can help you there. I know a man."

"No. It is forbidden."

"It is forbidden?" asked Fernando. "It is forbidden to destroy the life of one to save the life of another?"

Bella shook her head. "It's over. My life is over. Do as you wish to me."

Fernando smoothed her hair and tucked the loose strands behind her ear. He ran his dirty finger along her cheek and dropped it to her neck. Then she allowed his hand to move to her chest. Bella shuddered at his touch, her breathing quickened, and she clamped her eyes shut tight.

Fernando rested his hand on her stomach.

"So precious," he whispered. "You carry a miracle inside."

Bella didn't reply.

"Why do you fear me?"

She opened her brown eyes, and he met her gaze with curiosity.

"You could have it all," he said. "Everything you need. Everything you desire."

"My life was over when I left Syria."

"No, no, no," said Fernando. "Your life has only just begun." He slid his hand away and traced the outline of her belly with his finger.

Bella tensed as his touch ran along the outside of her leg to her dirty toes, and then began its journey back up the inside of her thigh.

"The way I see it, Bella, you are at a crossroads, a junction, if you will." He stopped at her knee and rested his hand. "One path leads to certain death, a long and painful death, in which you will not find martyrdom." His finger began its journey again, pulling with it the hem of Bella's torn dress. "The second path leads to a long and fruitful life with all the luxuries a girl like yourself could dream of, the softest bed you ever saw, the finest foods you ever ate, and the prettiest dresses money can buy. But only for you, you understand? You will bear *my* children and *my* children alone." His finger stopped at her stomach once more. He had revealed her nakedness beneath the dress.

"You carried this baby from Syria?" he asked.

Bella nodded. She knew it was a lie. She knew the child was his; it could only be his.

Fernando bent to her and began to kiss her neck with soft, gentle touches of his lips on her skin.

Small tears leaked from Bella's eyes and ran freely into her hair. She heard him inhale her scent, felt him feel her breast, and tasted his foul breath that hung heavily in the air.

"Tell me, Bella," he whispered. "Tell me what path you

choose and I will see to it that you get everything you deserve."

Fernando positioned himself on top of her, forcing her legs apart with his knee.

"Of course, for you to get what you desire, in return you must give me what I desire."

Bella felt him, hard against her body, but was unable to move.

Fernando bent to whisper in her ear. "I can be soft and gentle if you let me. I can make you happy."

She felt sick. Her throat had closed with fear and panic. She tried to speak, but no words came.

"Tell me which path you choose, Bella."

Fernando's breathing had quickened. He pressed into her in a slow rhythm.

"Bella, give me what I want," he said. "Look how far I've brought you." He kissed from her neck to her ear. "I can take you all the way."

"I..." Bella began. Her voice was raspy from her bone-dry throat.

"Yes?" whispered Fernando, pressing harder and breathing faster.

"I choose..."

Fernando gave a soft groan. "Choose life, Bella."

Bella opened her mouth to finish her sentence, but a small vibration from Fernando's pocket pulled him away. He sat up, and Bella saw his eyes widen with anger and frustration at the incoming call.

He pulled the phone from his pocket, hit the green button to connect the call, and sat back on his haunches, straddling Bella so she could not escape.

"Tell me you have him."

5

THE LESSER OF TWO EVILS

"ALL UNITS ABORT," CALLED MELODY INTO HER RADIO. "I repeat, all units abort. It's a trap. We're compromised."

"Who would have done this?" said LadyLuck; tears streamed from her eyes.

"Let's get out of here, Ladyluck," said Melody. "Take the stairs, it'll be quicker."

Ladyluck couldn't peel her eyes from Sharp's body.

"I said, let's *move*," said Melody, grabbing Ladyluck's arm and pulling her towards the door. She hit the push-to-talk button on her radio again. "The safe house is compromised. Wait for further instructions."

One short, sharp message returned with confirmation that mobile two had received and understood the message. "Copy that," said Derby.

"Down," said Melody, pushing Ladyluck towards the stairs.

"But what about Tenant and Jess?"

Melody stopped and took a quick look up the stairs to the roof.

"Stay here and scream if anyone comes," said Melody. She

checked the digital readout on the decrepit elevator. "The lift is on the ground floor. Keep an eye on that readout. If it starts to climb, shout for me. If you hear anyone on the stairs, shout for me. You got that? Anyone at all."

Ladyluck hugged herself and stared at the floor.

"Ladyluck, did you hear me?"

She looked up at Melody.

"Anyone comes and you call," said Melody. "I'll be right there. I'm not going far."

Ladyluck gave an almost imperceptible nod and blinked away the tears that had begun to pool in her eyes.

Melody sprang up the little stairwell. At the top was a small door with a push-bar fire exit handle and a tiny frosted glass window with steel mesh reinforcement. The glass was old, scratched and dirty. Melody couldn't see through it.

Pulling her Sig from her waistband, Melody loaded a round. She nudged the handle, and the door opened effortlessly.

The rooftop was covered in terracotta tiles with a thick layer of dust. Fresh footprints led from the door to the low wall that ran around the edge of the building.

"Ladyluck, are you still there?"

There was a brief pause then a scared voice came back. "I'm here, but hurry. I don't like it."

"Okay, just hang in there."

Melody stepped out onto the tiles. The prints weren't clear. It was as if someone had walked from the stairs to the wall and back several times, each time along the same route, and each time making an individual footprint harder to read.

She checked left and right, but the rooftop was empty. Keeping to the pre-made footprints to avoid making her own, Melody walked to the parapet wall and glanced down at the road below.

The car was gone.

"Shit."

A few moments later, she was bounding down the stairs and found Ladyluck stood rooted to the same spot, her eyes firmly on the elevator readout.

"Let's go," said Melody. "Stay behind me."

"What did you see?" asked Ladyluck, as she followed Melody onto the stairs.

Melody turned back to her and held her index finger to her lips to quiet her then continued to sidestep down the stairs with her back to the wall. They found the foyer empty. Melody pulled Ladyluck to one side of the two main doors.

"When we get outside, we need to run, okay?"

"Run?" said Ladyluck. "But where? Why? The car-"

"The car is gone," said Melody.

"What's happened?" asked Ladyluck, beginning to panic.

"Mobile two, come back. Do you receive?"

"Loud and clear, Mills," said Derby.

"The safe house is compromised. Avoid at all costs. We lost Reg and Jess, and we're running blind."

"Copy that," came Derby's reply. "Do you have an RV point?"

"We'll find you. Radio silence from here on in," replied Melody. "Emergency calls only."

She clipped the radio to her belt and looked Ladyluck up and down.

"You're going to need to lose those," said Melody, gesturing at Ladyluck's heels.

"These?" said Ladyluck. "But everything I had was in the car."

"Well, the car's gone, so you need to lose them."

Ladyluck gave an indignant groan and removed her shoes one at a time. She stood with them in her hand, her handbag hanging neatly off her shoulder.

"Where are we going to go?" she asked. "What's happened to the others?"

Melody peered around the corner at the doors, and then faced Ladyluck. "Reg and Jess are missing. We can assume that whoever took them was responsible for Sharp's death. Seeing as the car has gone too, we have to assume the driver was in on this too, and that Ferez knows our position. They probably came down the stairs with Reg and Jess while we took the lift up."

"But who-?"

"Whoever you contacted to arrange the cars and the apartment is in on this too, so that seems like a good place to start. Who was it?"

"I just have a number. Everything is on my laptop."

"In the car?" said Melody.

Ladyluck shrugged and held her hands palm out to indicate that she wasn't carrying anything but her bag and her shoes.

"You remember who your contact was?"

"It was a safe number. We only use trusted sources from the database. I didn't just find them on the internet," said Ladyluck, her tone becoming defensive and irritated.

"You ran checks? They were qualified?"

"Yes, of course. Jackson gave us the contact. We haven't had any issues before."

"Ladyluck, do you trust me?" asked Melody.

"Do I have a choice?"

"Right now, you have *two* choices," said Melody. "You can stay here and hope they don't come back."

"Or?" asked Ladyluck, dreading the next option.

"You can trust me. But it's going to be dangerous."

———

Harvey didn't watch the man fall to his death. He didn't even imagine the man's body being torn apart and spread across the jagged rocks for the bloody, red sea to consume. Instead, Harvey strode casually to the black rental SUV, opened the door and looked inside.

An old smartphone sat in the centre console under the overspilling ashtray. A cable ran from the cigarette lighter to the glove compartment where Harvey found a small photograph printer and a pack of photo paper. A few empty drink cans and sandwich wrappers littered the car floor, and all the surfaces had a layer of cigarette ash.

He took the phone and scrolled through the recently dialled numbers. There was only one number. Harvey hit the green button to initiate a call.

"Tell me you have him," came the answer.

"This stops now," said Harvey.

"Ah, Mr Stone," replied the voice. "You met my friend, I see."

Harvey recognised the voice of the tall man that had approached him on the beach months earlier. The whistle of a gentle breeze crackled through the phone's tiny speaker.

"I told you once before, I'm not interested in working for you. Consider this the second and last warning. There won't be a third, Ferez."

"Ah but, Mr Stone, a man of your talents is wasted on that little farm of yours. You could be so useful. What is it you grow there anyway? Memories?"

"If I'd have known you were going to pester me with pictures of your dirty little hobbies, Ferez, I'd have cut your throat the first time I met you."

Ferez gave a soft laugh. "I believe next time, Mr Stone, you won't have a choice *but* to help me."

"What's that supposed to mean?"

"You are a man who is guided by his moral compass, are

you not?" said Fernando. "You just can't help yourself, can you?"

Harvey didn't reply.

"I imagine, in your childhood, you were the boy who defended the little ones against the bullies. Am I right, Mr Stone?"

Harvey didn't reply.

"You're remembering it now, aren't you? All those sweaty tumbles with other prepubescent boys. You enjoyed the looks on their surprised faces, didn't you? You defended the wimps who lacked the courage and strength to fight their own battles. You enjoyed the power it gave you to overcome the selfish little boys." Fernando paused. Harvey's mind filled with featureless faces of his childhood that he'd destroyed and left behind.

"But most of all, Mr Stone," Fernando continued, "I believe you enjoyed the fear, the smell of the hunter becoming the hunted, the predator becoming the prey. There's a beast inside you, Harvey, and you need to exercise it."

A silence filled the airwaves between the two men.

"I'm right, aren't I, Harvey?" Fernando's tone took on a cruel, discriminated timbre. "Your silence is louder than you credit it for. You don't scare *me*, Harvey Stone. You won't smell my fear. You won't look into *my* eyes and allow the beast you nurture so lovingly inside your soul to grow and rise up. It won't strike *me* down, Harvey. You're no better than the bullies themselves.

"Is that right?" replied Harvey.

"You condescend me, Harvey?" said Fernando. "You talk as if you're surrounded by an indefeasible wall that nobody can climb, as if the beast inside chaperons you as you amble through your wasted life."

Harvey didn't reply.

Fernando had worked himself up. His breathing had quickened, and Harvey imagined his dark eyes widening with adrenaline.

"You'll come, Harvey," he continued. "You'll come when I ask you to come. You'll do as I ask, beast or no beast."

"Have you finished with the speeches?" asked Harvey.

"There's a hole in your defences, Harvey," said Fernando. "There's a hole so big I could park my boat in it."

"So it's a stalemate then," said Harvey.

"It seems that way. But whose move is it?"

"I don't care whose move it is, Ferez," said Harvey. "I already explained once; it ends here. Find someone else to do your dirty work."

"Oh, but I want *you*, Harvey Stone," said Fernando. "I need you, and I'll have you. I believe *you* called *me*. So that makes it my move, does it not?"

Harvey didn't reply.

"Start the clock, Mr Stone." Harvey almost heard the grin on Fernando's face in the shadow of his crooked nose. "Start the clock because this will be a move to remember."

———

"An old friend," said Fernando, as he disconnected the call and pocketed his phone. "I think you will meet him soon. I hope so."

Bella didn't reply. She gazed up into the sky at the white clouds that rolled overhead, free.

"Have you decided which path you will take, Bella?"

Bella lowered her gaze to look at Fernando.

"I have thought about it," she murmured softly.

"And?" pushed Fernando. "Do you choose death?" He reached behind him for his knife. "Or do you choose life?"

Fernando was perfectly silhouetted by the sun. His face

was lost in black shadow. The slightest cock of his head as he waited for her to answer was the only sign she could read.

"If I choose death..."

"Yes?" said Fernando. He span the knife in his hand and then rested the sharp point on her stomach.

"If I choose death, how will it be?" she asked. Her breathing turned hard and fast as she sucked in her stomach away from the blade.

"Slow," said Fernando. "Just like I told you."

"But how?" she asked. "With that?" She lowered her eyes to the knife.

Fernando shrugged.

"Maybe," he said. "Maybe a little with the knife, maybe a little with the water. I can be very creative, you know."

"And you will do it here? Now?" she asked.

"No," said Fernando with a cruel laugh. "This is no place to die. Think of the blood. Who will clean it all up when you're gone?"

The boat rocked as the strengthening wind picked up.

"And my baby?"

"Your baby?" he said. "You think I am an animal?" He seemed to grow angry at the statement. "Your baby will not suffer, if you live or if you choose death. But you are testing my patience, Bella. If you choose life, you will go to see my friend. He will take care of everything, and you will return to me clean. But if you choose death, it will be *your* choice, and therefore, you will be the murderer of your own child."

"But, not-"

"There's no buts, Bella," spat Fernando. "I'm offering you more than you ever dreamed of when you left that hole you came from. You dreamed of England, but what do you think you would get? A house, a car, a job? You people make me sick. There's no house waiting for you, no car, no job. You would be sheltered and fed, and that is all, while you wait in the system to be processed like a dog. Are you a dog, Bella?"

"No."

"What I am offering you, you must understand, is far beyond what England has to offer a refugee. You are a refugee, are you not?"

Bella nodded.

"A house, it is a nice house, with a garden where you will plant flowers and a kitchen that you will keep clean and cook in. You can cook, can't you, Bella?"

She nodded once more.

"You will have freedom, money to go shopping and buy clothes and food." He paused for a moment. "Money to buy clothes and food for our children."

"Our children," she repeated.

"Our children," said Fernando. His voice had calmed and softened as if coercing her with his gentle side. "Our children will be beautiful, Bella. Two boys and one girl. Two to carry my name and one to carry your beauty."

Bella turned her head to one side and stared out to sea. She quickly became mesmerised by the rolling tide and sideways sky.

Fernando reached down and smoothed her hair once more.

"Bella," he whispered, "from the day I first saw you, I knew. Such a pretty thing, far prettier than the other girls. Your mother was pretty too, yes?"

Bella didn't reply. She held the thoughts of her mother at bay in the depths of her mind, while hope showed itself in fleeting glimpses of what could have been, and what still might come.

"And you are strong, with a heart like a lion, yes?"

She turned to face him.

"We would marry then?" she said, as if the realisation of having children had only just fallen into place.

"We would marry, yes," replied Fernando. "You would be my wife, and I would be so proud, Bella."

"But I have to give you what you want?"

"And I have to give you what you want in return, Bella. I will provide. You will not go without. You will not be hungry, and you will bathe in soap and creams, and lie in the softest sheets."

"And what do you want from me?"

"There are many things I want, Bella," said Fernando, as he once again lowered himself on top of her. "But one thing at a time. I do not want to fight. I do not want to take." He stared into her brown eyes. "I want you to give it to me freely, as a man's wife should."

Fernando wiped a tear from Bella's eye and kissed her cheek. She lay still, unable to move, and unwilling to try.

"Do you choose life, Bella?"

She nodded. The small movement of her head sealed her fate, and Fernando smiled.

6

ROOFTOP RODEO

"WHERE ARE WE GOING?" ASKED LADYLUCK, AS SHE
stopped running and fell in behind Melody, who was peering
around the corner of a wall.

"We need to find mobile two. They have all our gear," she
replied.

"Can't we just chance getting them on the radio?" asked
Ladyluck. "Just once. My feet are getting torn to shreds."

Melody turned and looked at her feet. "Are they
bleeding?"

"Not yet," replied Ladyluck. "But-"

"When we get deeper into the backstreets, we'll be able
to slow down. But right now, we know that someone is out
there with Reg and Jess. We don't know how many there are,
or how heavily armed they are, but what we do know is that
they aren't afraid to kill."

"You think we'll find them?" asked Ladyluck. "Tenant, I
mean, and Jess?"

"It's been less than twenty minutes. Given the traffic in
Athens, they can't be more than three miles away, and given

that the people we're after operate from the boatyard, it's a safe bet that they've been taken there."

"So why are we running away from the boatyard into the city?"

Melody exhaled with frustration and put her hands on her hips.

"Because, Ladyluck," she said, "you have no weapons training or field experience. And you have no shoes. I have a handgun with one magazine. We need to find Derby so I can off-load you and get some hardware."

"Off-load me?" said Ladyluck. "So I'm slowing you down, am I?"

"Not really, Ladyluck. But trust me, if there was even the remotest possibility that I could take you into the boatyard so you could talk them to death while I escaped with Reg and Jess, we'd be running towards it and not away from it. But as it stands, you're an MI6 *researcher*, you're one of the team, and I'm not going to lose anyone else."

Ladyluck nodded at the assessment, and Melody turned back to the corner of the building.

"Do I talk too much?" asked Ladyluck.

Melody closed her eyes and took a breath.

"I mean, I can stop if you want. I just talk when I'm nervous. I don't really know why."

Melody turned back to her, ready to snap, when the front end of a black saloon car began to turn into the street.

"Move." Melody dragged Ladyluck around the corner into the side street, then pushed her into the entrance porch of an old shop with a boarded up doorway.

"Is that them?" asked Ladyluck. "Did they see us? Do you think they have Tenant in the car?"

Melody drew her Sig and ignored the questions. The sound of the engine approaching grew louder and the car's suspension squeaked on the rough cobbled street. Melody had noticed the sound on the journey from the airfield.

"It's them. Keep back," said Melody.

The car slowed then stopped, but the engine continued to run. They seemed to be waiting for something. Melody didn't dare to look around the corner. The car could only be ten metres away at the most, and they had nowhere to run. She studied the boards across the doorway.

"Ladyluck, see if you can open the door."

"It's boarded up," she replied. "How-"

A bullet ricocheting off the ground two feet in front of them cut her off.

Melody caught a glimpse of light from a nearby rooftop.

A scope.

She turned, shoved Ladyluck out of the way and planted a heel kick firmly into the door beside the lock. The old wooden frame splintered and the door crashed into the wall behind.

"Go. Now." Melody pushed Ladyluck into the dark space.

She glanced behind her in time to see another glint of light in the scope. Another round took a chunk of concrete off the building above her head. Dust and stones rained down, and she heard the car's engine rev.

Melody shut the door as best she could, and grabbed the top of an old wooden dresser.

"Help me," she called to Ladyluck. "Pull it over."

The pair heaved on the piece of old furniture, and let it crash to the floor. Then, seeing what Melody was trying to do, Ladyluck joined her in pushing it against the broken door.

"Now go," said Melody. "Look for a back door."

The boarded door began to splinter with holes and they heard the slamming of car doors. Then the door began to bang as men on the other side called to each other.

"There's no back door," said Ladyluck. "We're trapped."

"The stairs. Go."

The pair bounded up the four flights of stairs and heard the splintering of wood and crashing below, just as they broke out onto the roof.

Melody ran to the edge and looked across at the neighbouring rooftop. It was only a two-metre gap but at least a three-metre drop.

"No," said Ladyluck. "I can't do that."

Melody ripped a piece of timber off an old wooden pallet and forced it between the door handles.

"That should buy us some time," she said, just as the sniper found them on the roof and another bullet bounced off the doors.

"Damn it," she said, diving to the ground. "Can't we catch a break here?"

The two women rolled to the parapet wall that ran around the edge of the rooftop. The doors began to splinter as the men behind them fired into the wood.

"Handguns," said Melody. "That's a Glock."

"You can tell?" asked Ladyluck.

"Remember how I said you had two choices, Ladyluck?" said Melody, aiming at the doors, ready to take down whoever broke through.

"I chose wrong, didn't I?" replied Ladyluck.

"You can't change that now," said Melody. "But you do now have two more choices. The first one isn't great."

"And the second one?"

Melody glanced back at the low wall they would need to jump to reach the neighbouring building. "Even worse."

"No, Melody. I can't," said Ladyluck.

"Do you want to stay here and let whoever that is take you?" said Melody. "It's just a jump. It's not far. Just land and roll. You did gymnastics at school?"

"Twenty years ago, Melody."

More gunshots tore through the wood, then a boot burst through.

"You have seconds to decide, Ladyluck," said Melody, scrambling to her feet.

Immediately, a wild shot from the rifle on the far rooftop pinged off the parapet wall. Ladyluck moved into a crouch and peered behind her.

"Don't worry about him. He hasn't come close once," said Melody. "Are you ready?"

The wood that Melody had wedged between the door handles began to crack with the weight of the men ramming it from behind.

Ladyluck stood.

Another wild shot sang through the air close by.

"We're going to run and jump. Right foot on the wall, land with both feet, and roll. You got that?" said Melody, reaching for Ladyluck's hand.

The door finally burst open to their right.

"Now," screamed Melody. She pulled Ladyluck the first few steps. As soon as her right foot hit the wall, she let go and pushed off with everything she had, clearing the gap easily and landing with both feet. She tucked her head and rolled on one shoulder straight back up to her feet. Then she dove for cover into the open staircase.

Chancing a look back, Melody saw Ladyluck stood frozen with one foot on the parapet wall, her face a picture of fear, bewilderment and pure horror.

A man appeared behind Ladyluck, forced her arms behind her back then covered her mouth with his hand. Another man appeared, aimed his MP-5 at Melody and let off a three-round burst.

The last thing Melody saw before she made her escape down the stairs was a blow to Ladyluck's head, knocking her senseless. Her knees buckled, and she fell like a rag doll into her captor's arms.

———

Harvey was agitated.

Boon sensed his master's unrest and retreated to the bedroom to curl up on the warm bed, something Melody never allowed, but Harvey never noticed.

The two photos sat side by side on the coffee table. They seemed to stare at Harvey, almost beckoning him. He stood and opened the door to the wood burner, picked up two small logs to keep the fire going for a while, and then shut the door.

Harvey loitered by the fire for a few seconds then reopened the door and cast the two photos inside with the logs. He shut the burner and peered through the glass as the heat immediately took hold of the polyethene coating and began to melt, turning the already agonised faces into warped and perverted faces of horror.

He took his place on the couch once more and stretched out. The peace and quiet of their French home had been a dream of Harvey's for many years, and laying on his couch in total silence, except for the crackling and occasional hiss of the burning wood, had all been a part of that dream.

He'd often imagined how his future life would be during the times he'd sat waiting for a target, in the dark corner of a house, an alleyway, or a park. The hours had been long and silent with only his thoughts for company. His dreams of the house in France had accompanied him on so many of those occasions. And now, the dream had finally come true.

Except it hadn't.

Two voices sang in his head. Two faces haunted his imagination. His perpetual need to stand up to bullies tickled the nerves in his fingers; they twitched of their own volition. The movement caught Harvey's eye as if they belonged to someone else. He clenched his fist, closed his eyes, and tried to focus on the crackling and popping wood.

But the voices of the two beaten and abused girls in the photos chorused in his ear. Their faces morphed into one within the confines of his imagination. The photos were now one, and black and white as if ancient. Tears were the only movement in the scenes.

Harvey had seen it all before, pain, suffering, abuse. He'd seen suffering, instigated pain, avenged violence, and delivered retribution in too many cold, hard and drawn out deaths. Each murder was dispatched with the precision of a surgeon to ensure that the victim's last moments were filled with the misery that their own victims would endure for the remainder of their lives.

The photo in his mind now played like a showreel. The scene remained the same, but the faces changed like credits on a screen.

He remembered them all too well.

They haunted his dreams still. He occasionally woke in a sweat; not through guilt, he understood that his victims had all deserved every ounce of misery they suffered. But his dreams were fuelled by his hatred, a reminder of the good that he'd done, and the peace that he'd brought to others.

Recently, the dreams had become heavier and more vivid as if he was reliving the killings, and now, those twisted characters entered Harvey's waking mind through the medium of the two photos. The man he'd skinned alive. The man he'd glued down and whose stomach he'd slit open. The perverted rapist Harvey had buried alive with nothing but a hosepipe to encourage a futile glimpse of hope in the dying man's mind. The gargled chokes of a college lecturer who had abused his position; he'd walked into Harvey's trap as a fly might land in a web. Harvey had pinned him to the ground in a morbid crucifix with stakes that Harvey had carved while he waited. The man had slowly drowned in his own blood from the slightest of nicks to his windpipe from Harvey's blade. All of their screams howled inside Harvey's head.

In the past, long before France had become a reality, his dreams had woken him as a calling. Each target had satiated his thirst for retribution. But only for a while.

A temporary fix.

Harvey swung his legs off the couch, let his head fall into his hands, and forced the screams and tortured faces from his mind's eye. A method that had worked before had been to concentrate on the good things, the beach, his home, Melody and Boon. Melody had been a blessing for him. He'd never imagined he'd deserved someone like her, someone who knew about his past and understood him, or at least tried to. They'd started a life together which seemed to have eased the haunting dreams for a while. But now that the home in France and their lives together had become normality, the itch in his conscience had awoken the beast inside.

He reached for his phone and hit redial. He only ever called Melody, so her number was the only number on the list; she answered on the second ring.

"Hey handsome, I can't talk right now," Melody answered, sounding rushed. "Everything okay? You don't normally call at this time."

"Yeah, it's quiet here," said Harvey. "Can you run some checks for me on a number?"

"Ah, Harvey, we're right in the middle of a case. Can it wait?"

"I guess," said Harvey. "I just keep getting messages from a number. I thought you might be able to get me a location."

"As soon as I'm back in the office maybe, but hey, listen, I have to go," said Melody.

"Where are you?" asked Harvey.

"We've been through this, I can't talk about it. But I'll make it up to you when I get home, okay?"

Harvey didn't reply.

"Okay, stay out of trouble. See you soon."

Melody disconnected the call.

The light outside was slowly giving way to the night. The birds that tuned the peace had quietened, and the warm air from the wood burner seemed thick with memories in their small house. He thought of Melody and wondered what she was doing, what case she was working on. She had been an excellent operative, a highly skilled sniper, and a born leader. She never quite managed to think like a criminal, but instead, she was able to feel as they do, using some kind of criminal empathy that allowed her to be one step ahead. Harvey was proud of her. The frequent trips to London to work a case had been her own need. Much like Harvey, Melody had an itch and Harvey just couldn't stand in her way; he couldn't stop her from scratching it.

It was fully dark when the phone he'd found in the car earlier that day pinged a single sustained chime. Harvey reached for his leather jacket, pulled the phone from his pocket, and clicked on the message displaying another photo. This time the image resided on the phone. This time the man had gone too far.

Harvey turned away from the poor girl in the photo.

It was then that his own itch returned with a vengeance.

———

As land grew nearer, Bella's heart grew heavier. When the sound of the engine died down, and Fernando coasted the boat to a stop beside the dock, her body tensed. The realisation of her situation became a reality. It wasn't the empty boatyard or Fernando's smiling face behind the Perspex at the boat's controls, it was the massive expanse of Athens that spread out before her. The city was a sea of dirty white buildings wrapped in the arms of tall hills and mountainsides.

Escape now would be impossible. Where would she go? She didn't know the language; she knew only Arabic and the little English she had learnt. Being alone didn't scare Bella, being alone would be welcomed, being alone was better than giving her body to Fernando and his pig breath.

Somewhere in the city, she would spend the rest of her days and bear the children of her captor. Somehow, through all the turmoil, the loss and grief she had endured so far, it was possible that it would be a better life than she would have in England.

Bella took a breath. As Fernando stepped up to the dock and tied the bowline, she too stepped up, disembarking of her own fruition as if she was free to make those choices now. She stopped and waited for Fernando so as not to anger him.

"Welcome to my city, Bella," said Fernando. "I hope we will both be very happy here."

Bella stared at the city before her, and then back to the sea. She knew she would never see Turkey, or her friend, again. But the next step she took would be a step into a new life.

Freedom.

"Is it far?" she asked. "Your house?"

Fernando finished tying the boat to the dock and came to stand beside her.

"No, it is *our* house, Bella," said Fernando. "I want you to start to think like that. I want you to make the house your own house." He turned her roughly towards him. "I want you to be happy, Bella."

"Is it close?" she asked. "I would like to sleep."

"It is not far, and you can bathe and sleep as you wish

soon. We will be home in a while. I have a busy day tomorrow, but when I am done, I will show you the city."

"What is there to do here?" asked Bella. "Do you have places to walk?"

"There are many places to walk, many thousands of years old."

"Thousands of years?" asked Bella. "It is an old city?"

"One of the oldest" replied Fernando. "Do you see the big hill in the centre of the city?"

Bella nodded.

"This is the Acropolis. It is a marvellous construction, and surrounding it are churches and buildings and statues, with fine restaurants and wine."

"Wine?" said Bella. "I cannot drink wine."

"Then I will drink it for you," replied Fernando. "But you will love the food, and I will teach you to cook the way the local people do."

"You was born here?" asked Bella.

"No, Bella, I was not. I was born in Portugal, but I moved here when I was a child."

"Por-tu-" said Bella, trying to pronounce the word.

"Port-u-gal," said Fernando. "It is close to Spain but prettier." He gave her a little wink.

"Do you miss Por-tu-?"

"I remember few things about my home. Most of my memories are here in Athens." Fernando placed his hands gently on her shoulders and turned her to face the hills on the south side of the city. "It was in those hills that I used to walk with my uncle, and in the sea below where I learned to swim and to catch fish."

"Then," began Bella, "you are refugee also?"

Fernando's face hardened at the comment. "No, I am not like you, Bella." He seemed to spit the words out. "We had everything we needed, my family, but bad fortune."

"You ran," said Bella, "like me. We both ran. You are refugee."

"My father was killed. I did not run from a war into the arms of *anyone* who would take me. I came here to live with my uncle and to seek my fortune."

Bella lowered her head and closed her eyes.

"*My* family will be dead now, and I also did not run into the arms of just *anyone* who would take me, like you say. I *had* no choice."

"Well," said Fernando. His voice softened. "You have a choice now. The city is yours."

Bella opened her mouth to talk, but Fernando pulled away and answered his phone.

"Yes, boss," he began. "I am here now in Athens."

Fernando opened a door to a small building with what looked like boat engines in front of it and pieces of wood laying on the ground. Bella walked behind him into the building, and before Fernando had the chance to stop her from following, she saw the people inside. But they weren't just refugees. Alongside the refugees were white people. By their clothes, their faces, their hair, they were English, and they were chained to the walls. They were clean as if they had only just been taken there, not like Bella, who had grown used to being dirty, or the refugees, who cowered in the corner of the room.

A small part of Bella wanted to go and sit with the people she had travelled with for so long, to share the final leg of the journey with them. But she was different now.

She belonged to Fernando.

The white man croaked something. Her mouth fell open in pity, and the anguished looks of appeal on the faces of the man and two women were all too familiar for Bella.

But Fernando had seen her. He shoved her hard, back out

of the room and into the night with an angry look. He followed, locking the door behind him.

A part of Bella wanted to know who he was talking to, who his boss was, and what he was like. But the numbed and deadened part of her didn't care. His boss would be the man who had the money Bella's family had gathered for her to take the journey to England.

Her father had sold most of what they had, aware of the approaching army and the trail of destruction, and fully aware that someone as young and pretty as Bella would not stand a chance against the cruel soldiers. They would take what they wanted and leave the remains with nothing but a dead family and no chance of escape.

"How can you say that?" said Fernando. His voice raised as if his boss had triggered his defences. "*I* brought them from Syria, and *I* will get them to England. I've done it before, and I will do it again."

Bella thought of the others she'd travelled with and wondered what chances of life they really had. In the back of the boat, in the darkness, they had spoken often. But it seemed as if they had been brainwashed. There had been no doubt that England would be like a haven for them with free food, money and a roof over their heads.

Bella had been the one to question the truth. Bella had listened to them with their dreams of beautiful clothes. Omar, the silent man who had sat in the corner, had even spoken of getting a car so he could drive to see the famous green hills in the English countryside, where food grows in rich fields that roll on for as far as the eye can see.

He'd silenced again when Bella had asked him why England would give free food, money and homes to refugees. She hadn't doubted that England would help. But she was aware that it would be a hard time, and perhaps many years before they could have jobs that might pay enough for them to be independent.

"So how come you are here?" the older lady had asked.

Bella had replied, "Because no matter how hard the work is, no matter the suffering, there will be life and a future. I just cannot describe that future. It is all too uncertain."

Fernando was in the midst of an argument with his boss. His raised voice snapped Bella back to the present.

"You cannot replace *me*," he said. "I have helped you from the start. The contacts we use are all my own, not yours."

A pause.

"Yes, you funded the boats, and I agree; you also supplied the bribe money. But without my contacts, not one of them would have made it through."

Fernando silenced while his boss seemed to give him an ultimatum.

"Trust me," Fernando replied. "I will get them out of Athens and into the UK, and if I don't, then fine, we will go our separate ways."

He was about to disconnect the call when his boss seemed to have one more thing to say.

"Yes?"

Fernando's frown relaxed, and a broad smile spread across his face as if his skin was made of clay. His nose was the only feature that remained impassive to the news.

"How many of the interfering agents are left? How many do we need to worry about?" A pause. "Three?"

Bella wondered what he was talking about. How many of who were left? She continued to listen to the one-sided conversation.

"Two men and a woman?"

"I am about to send him one last photo," said Fernando. "He will be here by morning. He can't ignore me forever."

"Yes, I am sure." Fernando turned away and lowered his

voice, but Bella heard him whisper in the quiet night. "It will be perhaps the most tantalising photo yet. In the morning, Mr Stone will be our newest employee."

Fernando disconnected the call.

"Is there trouble?" asked Bella.

"No, Bella," replied Fernando, his smile still intact. "In fact, I think things just took a turn in the right direction."

"It *sounds* like trouble," said Bella.

"Ah, my sweet Bella," said Fernando. He smoothed her hair with a dirty hand. "Why don't you wait in the car?" He gestured at the silver Mercedes parked behind the workshop. "I have some business to take care of, and it's something that someone as pretty as you should not have to see."

7

ARRIVAL OF THE BEAST

FROM THE DOORWAY OF THE NEIGHBOURING HOUSE, Melody watched three men load Ladyluck into the back of the black Peugeot. Two climbed in either side of her, and the other took the front passenger seat. The sniper was nowhere to be seen, though he was clearly untrained and a poor shot. But if he saw Melody, he could easily give away her position.

The car pulled out slowly. Melody considered that several gunshots had been fired, and although the area was almost derelict, somebody could have heard them and called the police. The men had seemed unconcerned. Melody realised that she had, in fact, not seen another person or car since their arrival at the apartment building, other than the men and the black Peugeot.

She desperately needed to find Derby. She needed to find Reg. She also needed a weapon. But, first of all, she needed to get away from where she was.

Keeping to the backstreets, Melody meandered through the narrow alleyways in the general direction of the city centre, using the behemoth Acropolis as a guide. The further away from the industrial area she walked, the more people began to fill the streets. Cars became more frequent; at first, this put her on edge and caused her to slow down to study every individual. But after a while, the crowds grew busy enough for her to blend in. Thoughts of stopping in the quaint little stores or wandering the markets were far from her mind. Her focus was finding Derby, Reg and Jess.

Finding Reg and Jess wouldn't be too hard; Melody had a plan for that. But overcoming the gang on her own could be extremely difficult with just a handgun. Finding Derby would mean she would have her rifle, and she could then find a perch somewhere to pick them off by one by one.

While walking, she gave Derby a lot of thought, trying to empathise with him to work out where he'd be. If she was him and she had been told to wait in Athens until further notice, what would she do?

Given the fact that he had a vanload of equipment, including rifles, surveillance gear, computers, scanners, and satellite comms, Derby wouldn't leave the vehicle unattended. This gave Melody an idea. Derby wasn't a tech guy, but they all knew how to work the frequency scanners. If Melody were sat in a van full of tech gear waiting for someone to find her, she'd use the scanners to dial into the police channel and wait for the action.

Melody needed to create some action.

She came to the end of a street and turned left up a long hill. A tiny old church stood in the centre of the road, splitting the wave of tourists into two, left and right. The tourists merged again on the far side of the church, but the variance in the flow of foot traffic was an ideal spot for pickpockets.

Melody spotted them easily enough. Congregated around the edges of the junction were drug addicts, the jobless and the homeless, drinking cans of strong lager or cider, and smoking cheap cigarettes or joints. The pickpockets stood to one side of them, ever watchful.

Melody made herself an easy target.

She pulled a ten-euro note from her cargo pants and tucked it so that it was half in and half out of her back pocket. She walked past the intimidating crowd as if she were lost, turning herself around, and checking the streets signs. Then she walked on and waited.

Less than two minutes later, she felt the tug on her cargo pants and span on the spot to find the thief running away at a full sprint down the hill. He looked to be a skinny man, unshaven, with tattoos and a green mock army jacket.

"Stop, thief," she screamed, then pulled her Sig and placed two careful shots over the man's head harmlessly into the air. The thief ducked into a side road. Tourists dove for cover into shops and one local man fell off his bicycle in an effort to stop quickly. The busy street emptied in seconds.

As planned, it took less than a minute until she began to hear the sound of approaching sirens, so she made her exit into the shadows of a tiny side street. Once out of sight, Melody too ran at full speed away from the scene. She found the entrance to an apartment building between two tourist shops, sprinted up the stairs to the rooftop, and looked down at the street.

The police had arrived and had begun to question tourists, who described the events and illustrated their stories with wild gestures of their hands. A woman holding a child pointed in the direction of the pickpocket then mimed Melody firing her weapon. Another man pointed roughly in the direction that Melody had run. The policeman spoke into his radio.

That was when Melody's plan looked like it would fail.

From her vantage point on the roof above, she could see down at the intersection of four small streets. Near the church where she had fired the shots, more police congregated, and then a chief gestured at the officers. To Melody, it was clear what his instructions to his team were without hearing.

They were to check the surrounding buildings and go door to door.

Melody crouched behind a parapet wall for the second time that day, and seriously doubted her plan. She hadn't thought it through properly. It had been a hunch, and it was looking as though it might have been a terrible decision with dire consequences. She chanced another look down. There were two officers on her street stepping into the building beside hers. Melody estimated the time to search the four-story building; two apartments on each floor and then they would check the roof space, where they would look across and see Melody. Ten minutes, maximum.

A few tense minutes passed. Two more policemen were in the adjacent street, coming out of one building and straight into another. They spoke casually, seemingly bored. One of the cops smoked a cigarette. The other was overweight and disinterested. Melody hoped they represented a standard fitness level across all Athens police force. If she had to run, she might just stand a chance.

Melody heard banging on the roof access door of the neighbouring building. The door was locked. Maybe that would stop them. Maybe not.

She took another look over the wall to the street below. More police had joined the effort of checking the buildings. They were closing in.

But then she saw what she was looking for. Melody started for the stairwell just as the policemen broke through the door on next building. For the tiniest of moments, Melody held his surprised gaze. Then she ran.

"Edo," the first one called, immediately seeing her run.

He pulled his weapon and fired two rounds just as Melody dove into the stairwell. She landed painfully on her side, half rolling and half falling onto the first few steps. As momentum picked up, she continued to bounce hard on her back to the floor below.

Melody heard the shouts from above as she lay slightly dazed on the floor, winded and bruised. She bound down the remaining stairs, pulling her radio from her pocket. She had just one chance.

"Mobile two, stop where you are," she said and prayed that Derby had heard. She'd just kicked the hornet's nest, and if her timing was wrong, she was about to get stung.

Melody jumped the last few stairs. The jolt was like a dull kick to the fresh bruises on her back, but she carried on with gritted teeth and burst through the single entrance door onto the street.

A group of four policemen saw her, but it took them a few seconds to realise that she was their suspect. By the time they had engaged their brains, Derby had slammed the van brakes on and crawled alongside her. The side door slid open, and Melody fell into the rear cargo area.

A few sporadic gunshots dotted the back of the van, but Derby easily slid around a few tight corners and gunned the engine, leaving the unsuspecting police behind.

———

The ride in the taxi from the airport to Athens took around thirty minutes. Harvey sat in the front passenger seat, as he always did in taxis, and focused on the facts.

The girls in the first two pictures had clearly been beaten and abused, but the captors were obviously capable of a lot more, judging by the last photo. It had shown a girl surrounded by old boats on trailers hanging naked by her feet from the type of gantry that mechanics might use to hoist a boat from a trailer. Harvey pictured the girl. There was no need to open the phone to look at the photo again. What he'd seen was beyond abuse. It was an image he'd never forget.

Harvey asked the driver to stop as soon as the coast was in full view. He didn't carry a bag or a gun, or even his knife. Worse than that, Harvey didn't have a plan.

That would be his first port of call.

The sky was growing dark, and the sun began to sink into to the Mediterranean, lighting up the mountains that surrounded the city. The same mountains would help Harvey find where the captives were being held. Harvey had noticed that behind the girl in the last photo, the ridgeline of the peaks that cradled Athens was just in view. There was nothing particularly outstanding about the rocky features, but their shape would be distinct enough for Harvey to work out the rough direction of the boatyard. Then he would just need to wait and watch the activity.

He took a walk down to the beach and considered his options. The first pictures of the girls had been taken inside a boat, possibly a fishing vessel. It hadn't been a new yacht with a white fiberglass hull and stainless steel bimini, rails and stays. Instead, it had been a dark and dirty boat, possibly with nets and bundled up canvasses, and with random fishing gear dotted around. Harvey had an image in his mind of what he was looking for.

He remembered Ferez's statement.

"You have a hole in your defences so big I could park my boat in it."

At the coast, there was a large marina with expensive yachts and bay-liners for water sports. There were no old fishing boats moored there. He was in the wrong area.

Harvey had checked a map of Athens on the internet

before he had left France. He'd seen that the coastline was relatively short and that in the north and south, a small range of mountains sat like arms around the city. He'd also seen what looked to be dry docks or boatyards at both ends of the coast, the type of place where a mechanic might need a gantry to raise and lower a boat off a trailer.

Harvey studied the mountains to the north and to the south then took an educated guess at the location being at the north end of the coastline. The peaks looked right, and the gradient of the mountains seemed to match the image in his mind. But he wouldn't know for sure until he got there.

He acted like any other tourist walking along the coastline, carrying his leather biker jacket slung over his shoulder and wearing sunglasses. As he made his way north, he took in the sights, while passing groups of teenagers, couples and occasionally a foursome of retired people. Harvey assumed that they were visitors from the cruise ships that stood proudly in the port to the north.

Gradually, the tourist restaurants and souvenir shops became less frequent. Life on the streets began to quieten. Large cruise ships stood in line to dock at the port, patiently waiting for the hungry and cash-rich tourists.

It was as he passed the entrance to the docks that a flashing blue light ahead caught Harvey's eye. Two police cars and an ambulance sat outside what looked like an old rundown apartment building a few hundred yards along the road. Harvey crossed the street to be on the same side when he approached.

Four fat and lazy-looking policemen stood waiting beside their cars, smoking and talking loudly, each one fighting to be heard above the other with wild expressive gestures of their arms and faces. Then two men emerged from the building carrying a stretcher, which they loaded unceremoniously into the ambulance before closing the doors.

Harvey knew a dead body on a stretcher when he saw one. The childhood memory of his sister being carted out of his foster father's house had been ingrained into his mind. It was one of the catalysts for who he'd grown to be. Ironically, it was also the reason he found himself in Athens.

He approached the building as the convoy of emergency vehicles moved away. There was nothing to see from the outside, just an old dirty building opposite three rough and dirty boatyards.

Harvey walked to the corner of the building and looked up the hill at the receding police cars. In front of him was a perfect view of the mountains, clearly bearing the features he'd seen in the photo. He was in the right place.

All that remained was to identify which of the three boat-yards belonged to Ferez and had the refugees inside. For that, he'd need to find a high spot where he could sit and watch. Harvey glanced back at the dirty old apartment building that he'd just passed. It was ideal for his needs. Plus, something about it didn't sit right; four policemen had attended a crime in a deserted neighbourhood and then stood outside smoking while the EMTs had dealt with the body.

It had all seemed a bit too easy.

Harvey checked around him with a subtle glance left and right, then walked back to the entrance of the building. The names on the intercoms had faded to nothing, and a thick layer of dust lay on the granite floor of the foyer, recently disturbed.

Given the choice of a tiny elevator and the stairs, Harvey opted for the stairs, climbing straight to the top floor, where he was immediately hit by the stench of cat urine. The smell seemed to come from the apartment on the right. The door was open, and from a quick glance inside, Harvey saw that it, like the rest of the building, had been abandoned.

The apartment on the left had police tape across the door

but stood ajar. Harvey gave it a nudge, and let the door swing open. He listened for movement or breathing. A novice killer would have adrenaline coursing through his veins; it was the hardest thing to control. But he heard nothing. Harvey lifted the tape, stepped inside, and pushed the door closed quietly behind him. He waited for a full minute in silence before moving further. Old habits.

The view from the empty living room gave him a perfect view over the boat yards, exactly as he'd hoped. Though the light was fading, he could see that they were all individually fenced off with chain link fencing. A tiny strip of wasteland separated one from the next. Each boatyard had a collection of small buildings amid the random boats and vessels.

Then a familiar shape caught his eye. In the pale light, standing tall beside an old workshop building, he found the gantry that the girl in the last photo had been hanging from; a few old oil drums stood beside it, along with a wooden reel of what even at that distance, Harvey knew to be barbed wire.

"Found you," he whispered to himself.

———

"This is your home?" asked Bella, as she closed the door to Fernando's old Mercedes.

"No, Bella," replied Fernando. "This is *our* home. That's how I want you to think of it now, as our home."

Bella's heart sank a little. The house and garden walls were crumbling, and the bright blue window frames did little to bring any joy to the sorry-looking building. The terracotta roof sagged in the middle as if it would collapse in a strong wind, and the forecourt was strewn with leaves from nearby trees and rubbish that either Fernando had discarded or passers-by had dropped into the property; probably both, thought Bella.

Wild vines covered the front of the small one-story building, bearing red flowers, which were bright against the dirty white walls, but not bright enough to distract from the deep cracks than ran from the roof to the ground. The barred windows grinned at Bella's arrival. Bella wondered if the bars were to stop robbers getting in or people like Bella getting out.

The property stood at the centre of a steep hill, with houses spread out below and above. From the lofty heights of Fernando's house, the rows of buildings below seemed to occupy every available space.

"I like the view," said Bella.

"You wait until you see inside, my sweet," said Fernando. "It needs a little work, but I'm sure you'll manage just fine."

Fernando lifted the gate open, rather than swung it, and then waved for her to follow him to the front door.

I could run now, while his back is turned. It might be my last chance.

She glanced to her left back down the hill. So many alleyways, perfect for hiding.

"Bella?" said Fernando. "Are you coming?"

She turned back to him, nodded and feigned a smile, then followed obediently.

Inside, the house bore the aroma of dirty clothes, unwashed bodies and stagnant water. The smell seemed to warm the air. Bella forced the front door closed behind her, and had to turn sideways to move along the hallway past boxes of magazines, newspapers, lamps and all sorts of bric-a-brac. Fernando, it seemed, had hoarded everything he'd ever seen, bought or found.

She remembered clearly a discussion she'd had with her mother, during one of their chats.

"We might not have everything we want, Bella," her mother had said. "But your father works hard to make sure we have everything we need, and those things, we need to take care of so they see many years."

"But the other children have televisions," Bella had replied.

"Do not concern yourself with the things that other families have, Bella. When you walk into our home, you smell fresh clothes, clean floors, and homemade cooking. I have seen the houses of other families. They are no better than the vermin that feed from the garbage." Her mother had spoken with distaste.

Bella had found it odd that the families of her friends, who had more money than Bella's, would choose to live like that.

Fernando's house reminded her of her friend's house.

"Are you coming?" asked Fernando from the end of the hallway. "I want to show you the kitchen."

Bella snapped out of her memory, and dreaded seeing the state the kitchen.

"It needs a little cleaning, but can you see past that?" said Fernando. "Can you see yourself here with the children running around your feet?"

"And where will you be?" asked Bella. "While I am cooking and looking after the children?"

"I will be working, or relaxing after a hard day." He looked confused, as if her question had been rhetorical. "You will be happy here, Bella. I promise you."

"I would like to use the washroom," she said under her breath.

"I will show you," said Fernando.

"No," said Bella, a little too sharp. "No, I am sure I will find it."

The fact was that Bella could smell the bathroom above

the stale body odour, rotting food and stagnant water. She wasn't prepared, however, to walk into a bathroom quite so bad as it was. Bella immediately gagged as the stench clung to her throat. She ran from the tiny room and stomped into the kitchen.

"Bella?" said Fernando. "You look upset. What is wrong? Do you not like the house?"

Bella was incredulous at how Fernando could not see what she saw, or if he did, how he could even imagine that the hygiene was acceptable.

"I must say what I am thinking," she said, "or I will not say anything all."

"So speak, Bella," said Fernando. "You are free now, remember?"

"You..." She tried to sugarcoat the words, but there was no use. "You live like a *pig*, Fernando. You have insects crawling on the dinner things. You have *never* cleaned your toilet, and something, somewhere, has died inside this house. It is foul. I *cannot* live here."

She closed her eyes and waited for the attack.

Fernando crushed his cigarette into a dirty dinner plate with hardened food encrusted onto its surface. He spoke quietly but was clearly insulted.

"For somebody who has just escaped a war zone and lived in the very pits of trucks and boats being fed by whoever would feed you and drinking from a bowl like a dog," said Fernando, catching his breath as his temper began to soar, "you have a very big mouth."

"This is *filth*," Bella began, almost pleading.

"*This*," snapped Fernando, his index finger pointed into the air, "is your home. And this..." He spread his arms out as if presenting the hovel as some kind of grand palace. "Is your kitchen." He lit another cigarette and left the room leaving Bella staring at her feet, expecting another blow.

"Oh, and Bella?" Fernando continued, as he opened the front door to leave.

She looked up at him, ashamed of her ingratitude.

"If you do not like its present condition, you should clean it. I'll be back shortly, and I shall be hungry."

8

MORNING MONSTER

THE VAN DOOR SLAMMED. MELODY SAT BOLT UPRIGHT IN A panic. It took her a few seconds to realise where she was.

"Hey, you were out cold," said Derby, reaching from the driver's seat into the back of the van to pass Melody a coffee.

"What time is it?" she asked.

"It's morning, but more importantly, it's time we ditched the van. We were lucky to find this place to hole up in last night, but we can't go driving around the streets in it all day."

Melody moved from the nest she'd made between the boxes and flight cases, and sat on the wheel arch.

Barnet turned around from the passenger seat. "We did a few drive-bys yesterday. The place is deserted. It's like the tourists still plague the city centre, but that little industrial area is a ghost town."

"Yeah, I noticed that," replied Melody. "It's the perfect place to bring in a bunch of refugees. No-one is snooping around."

"It's not just refugees, Melody," said Derby.

"What do you mean?"

"I mean, yeah sure, it's the refugees that sit in the back of the truck and get driven across Europe. But you don't think that any enterprising people smuggler is going to leave money on the table, do you? He's not going to miss out on any opportunity to get a bit more bang for his buck."

"Drugs?" asked Melody. "Is that it?"

"I would imagine so. We've seen it before," said Barnet. "There's usually a guy that'll escort a bunch of refugees out of the war zone, guide them through Turkey and land them here in Athens or somewhere else in Europe for the final leg of the trip."

"At which point the refugees' options are minimal, and they'll do anything that's asked of them," Derby cut in. "I mean, Athens isn't exactly thriving, is it?"

"So," said Melody, falling in with what the two men were saying, "instead of being taken on the final leg of their journey as they had paid for-"

"They're given an ultimatum. Stay here, or become-"

"Mules," finished Melody. "These poor people have been through enough. They've lost their families and starved from hiding in trucks for months to get here."

"And the worst thing is, Melody, most get caught going into Britain and wind up being thrown in the slammer-"

"At Her Majesty's pleasure," finished Barnet.

"Do we have proof of this?" asked Melody.

"That's what Sharp and Gibson were doing. You don't think we'd be involved if it was just a people smuggling case, do you?" said Derby. "No, this lot are bringing in ten or twenty people every week, and if each one of them is carrying a kilo or two of heroin or coke, or both, each of the refugees would be worth a fair old amount to the smuggler."

"Heroin is about seventy pounds a gram on the streets of London, maybe more, give or take, and that's probably cut too. But seventy pounds times a thousand grams is-"

"Seventy thousand," said Melody.

"Multiply that by, let's say, ten refugees," said Derby.

"Seven hundred thousand," said Melody.

"Now factor in anything else they can carry or put inside them," said Barnet.

"That all sounds a bit far-fetched, boys," said Melody. "Don't you think?"

"Yeah, it does sound like a movie plot," said Barnet. "But think of it this way, each of those refugees pays ten or twenty grand to get through Europe and into Britain. What's that? One hundred grand, maybe two hundred? Now to some, that's a hell of a lot of money, to most in fact. But is it enough for someone to kill a couple of MI6 agents over?"

"Gibson and Sharp?" said Melody.

"Yeah, why kill them?" said Barnet. "Whatever they found and whatever the smugglers are doing is worth considerably more than a few hundred grand, isn't it?"

Barnet turned in his seat again and smiled at Melody.

"Why didn't the whole team know about this?" asked Melody. "Why were we all led to believe that it was just a people smuggling case?"

"It's all speculation, Melody," said Derby. "What we need to do is catch a real live mule in the hands of a real live smuggler. Then, and only then, can we link them to all the other mules we have locked up back home."

"No," said Melody, "you're missing the point."

"What point is that?" asked Barnet.

"Reg and Jess are *missing*, plus three other operatives. Rescuing *them* is our new objective. If we can take the smuggler out in the meantime, then fine, but our focus needs to be on getting the team back. With them, we'll stand a much stronger chance of taking the smugglers down."

"And you think we can just walk in there and rescue them, do you?" asked Derby. "You saw what they did to Gibson, and I know you saw what happened to Sharp."

"That's nothing compared to what I'm going to do to these bastards," said Melody.

———

"I told you to stop sending me photos," said Harvey into the phone. "For someone who says he knows me, you don't seem to know me very well, do you?"

"Good morning, Mr Stone," replied Fernando. "It's a shame, you know. She was such a nice girl. But you know how it is, in every game, there has to be a loser and there has to be a winner. We do not like to be losers."

"Is she dead?" asked Harvey.

"Maybe," replied Fernando. "But maybe not. She may have pulled through the night. They are strong, these people. They have suffered very much."

"Let them go, Fernando," said Harvey. He began to pace the room.

"Oh, but we're only just beginning. The game is just warming up."

"What is it you want, Fernando?"

"Straight to the point, eh? You're a man of few words."

Harvey didn't reply.

"I imagine you're holed up in some grotty little apartment building overlooking our little boatyard. Am I right, Mr Stone? Or can I call you Harvey? I imagine you followed the clues. Such a good dog, maybe I'll throw you a bone."

"Call me what you like, I'll be cutting your throat soon enough."

Fernando ignored the threat, and continued with his synopsis. "I also imagine that you found somewhere empty, easy to access with all the doors unlocked. Am I right, Harvey?"

Harvey didn't reply.

"And I imagine you wouldn't want to spend the night in a room that smells like cat piss, so you took the left side apartment."

Silence.

"I'm right, aren't I Harvey?" said Fernando with a chuckle. "I usually am, and you're so predictable."

Harvey immediately felt the trap. He began to search the other rooms.

"Have you checked the other rooms?"

Harvey sighed. "Of course."

"I hope my boys didn't make too much mess?" Fernando gave a soft groan. "Sorry about that. I did tell them to keep the place clean for our guests."

"Who was it?" asked Harvey, remembering the body bag.

"Oh, you know what? The name escapes me. I've always been bad at names," said Fernando. "Just one of those meddling men."

"Are you going to tell me where I come into all of this? It sounds like you and your boys have things wrapped up."

"Sadly not, Harvey. We have a truck leaving our little boatyard this afternoon and it's worth a considerable sum of money to us. But we still seem to have some loose ends that are trying to stop our little operation. So annoying, don't you agree?"

"Right."

"Well, we've exhausted our own resources, and I would like very much for my men to get back to work. Production cannot stop because of one little set back, you know."

"So?"

"Well, we didn't quite round them all up," replied Fernando. "A few slipped through the net, and we do like to do a proper job. No loose ends."

"And?"

"If you can stop the rest of *them*, then maybe *we* won't

have to hurt any more pretty girls." Fernando smiled. "It's a simple game, Harvey."

"How many?"

"Three. Not many for a man of your calibre. But the ones we've managed to capture so far don't seem to be very talkative, so we can't be too sure."

"And that's it, is it?" asked Harvey. "I stop the men, you get your truck out, and you leave me alone?"

"Something like that, yes."

"No, Fernando," said Harvey. "We need clear terms and conditions. It's a transaction. I stop the men, you get your truck out, and you leave me alone. Any deviation from the plan and it's game over."

"I can hear your mind ticking over," said Fernando. "You give away far too much. Perhaps that's why you rarely say anything. Am I right, Harvey?"

"Do we have a deal, Fernando?" said Harvey. "I don't have time for games."

"You think you can fool me with some sort of verbal agreement, hoping that I will relax, thinking that you will take these men down. But really, you're coming after me, aren't you? You want to free the refugees don't you? And by that admission, I'd say that you also want to kill me."

Harvey didn't reply.

"I'm right, aren't I?"

"Do we have a deal, Fernando?"

"Here's the deal. Bring me the bodies and get our trucks through, and I'll see to it that the refugees reach England, although I can't guarantee they'll all be completely unscathed. One, in particular is in a bad way. It's a shame, she's such a pretty thing, and our night security is a little bit...Well, let's just say he doesn't get out much, and the sight of her in such a weak and vulnerable state might just have been enough to send him over the edge. Do you catch my drift, Harvey?"

Harvey didn't reply.

"You can reach me on this number when you've made your choice. Oh, and by the way, Harvey, welcome to Athens. I knew you'd come eventually."

Fernando disconnected the call.

Harvey pocketed the phone and began to pace the room. The abandoned apartment building allowed him a birds-eye view of the boatyard. He saw the salvage boats lined up for scrap, the mobile gantry that the girl had been tied to, and what looked to be a workshop in the centre of the plot. The chain link fence that ran around the perimeter would be easy enough to scale, and there was enough vegetation in the wasteland surrounding the yard for someone to sit and watch.

Harvey began to formulate a plan. Save the refugees, and kill Ferez. If he had to go through with Ferez's demands to do so, then so be it.

He considered his approach.

If his old team were to launch an attack on the workshop, they would have placed a sniper up high, and then sent in a few men to coordinate an attack from all sides. It would help if Harvey knew who he was up against. Was it just a team of vigilantes? Was it an enemy of Fernando and his boss? A turf war, maybe? Or was it some kind of authority? The police would have helicopters and wouldn't be sitting around waiting for things to happen. Plus, the four lazy policemen Harvey had seen hadn't seemed too bothered by the body. Maybe the police were on the payroll.

Harvey stood over the bloodstained screed floor in the bedroom of the apartment and hit redial on the phone.

Fernando answered the call with a chirp.

———

"Harvey, so have you made your decision then?" said Fernando. "So quickly too. That's what I like to see."

Bella lay on her side with her back to Fernando, pretending to sleep and fighting back her stinging tears. She'd barely slept all night, kept awake by the evil presence of Fernando who lay beside her and his incessant drone.

Only a man with no conscience could sleep during times of such atrocities, she had thought.

She had remembered where she was as soon as she had awoken from one of few exhaustion-induced sleeps. The reality of her stupidity had hit her hard, just as the nasty smell of the bed sheets choked her throat.

Bella felt Fernando's wandering hand reach around and cup her breast and she fought not to open her eyes. At least if he thought she was sleeping, he wouldn't force himself on her again.

"Now, now, Harvey, there's no need for that kind of talk."

Whoever this man Harvey was, Fernando obviously thought he was a dangerous man. Bella clung to the hope that he would rescue her. She longed to be in that workshop with the other refugees and the people she had seen the night before. Although they had been tied and left in the dark, at least they were together.

"As long as our trucks can get out without being stopped, then I see no reason to worry about us hurting anybody else." Fernando paused as the voice replied. "No, Harvey. I want to see the bodies. This might be a game, but I make the rules."

Fernando pinched Bella. She opened her eyes with a start and rolled over to face him, so his hand was away from her chest.

"Let's make it interesting," said Fernando into his phone. "Our truck leaves at four pm. I want to see three bodies before midday. That gives you five hours to take care of them, or the truck will be slightly lighter, if you get my meaning."

Harvey didn't reply.

"There's not many rules in my game, Harvey." His hand moved to Bella's backside. "You finish them however you see fit." He paused again.

"Calm down, calm down, Harvey." Fernando began to stroke Bella's back. She shuddered at his gentle touch, somehow preferring it when he was rough and more genuine. She knew his soft touches were just for show, especially following his previous night's demonstration of power.

"Maybe once this is over, we can have a little chat. Who knows, you might like working with us."

Bella heard the phone's tiny speaker emitting the other man's voice. He sounded angry.

"Right now, you don't have the power to make those kind of statements, Harvey. You should remember that I have some very nasty men at my disposal, and one of those girls, in particular, will please the boys very much."

Fernando paused.

"That's right, Harvey, you stay silent. That's the best way."

Fernando lifted the bed cover and pushed Bella's head down. She resisted at first, but he grabbed her hair and pushed harder.

"Now I have your attention, Harvey. Bring me the bodies by midday today, or another girl dies. We have enough refugees; we can afford to lose one or two along the way."

Fernando disconnected the call and put the phone down beside Bella.

She looked up at him.

"Oh Bella," said Fernando. "You have a lot to learn."

He slid out of bed and walked naked to the door. "Unfortunately, today is a very busy day for both of us, so we will resume our lessons later."

Bella covered herself with the dirty covers.

"And what it is we are doing today?" she called out.

"You don't need to know the details, Bella. But know this, until you prove yourself to me, you shall either remain locked inside this house, or you'll stay by my side." He lowered his tone again. She was beginning to hate and fear his gentle tone as much as she hated his gentle touch. Cruelty usually followed both.

"I want to trust you, Bella," he continued. "I want you to be happy. But until I can trust you, I'm afraid I must insist that you stay by my side."

"Then you should tell me what it is I should do to make you trust me. Tell me what I should do and I will do them," Bella lied. "I want so much to be happy. I want to walk in the glorious hills and breathe the fresh air."

Fernando eyed her with caution then eased into his tight, thin-lipped smiled. "You just carry on doing what you did for me last night and this morning, and I'm sure we'll be just fine."

"This is what you like?" asked Bella, as innocently as she could fake it.

"This is what all men like, Bella. But you, my dear, are fortunate enough to be with a patient man who will teach you." He nodded as if even he believed his own words. "Just wait, Bella, your time will come. Now get dressed. We have a busy day."

"But I have only the clothes I was wearing," said Bella, "and they are ruined."

"So?" replied Fernando.

"So, I want to look my best for you. I want you to be proud, as I am." She mumbled the words and looked away at the barred window.

Fernando was silent for a moment then stepped back into the room. He pulled open the small wardrobe. On one side were his own clothes, a mix of various coloured shirts and pants. At the other end of the rail were three dresses. They were old, and not Bella's style.

"Choose one," said Fernando. "It is a gift to you, my Bella."

Bella wrapped the dirty bed covers around her and edged off the bed to look closer at the dresses.

"You should not cover yourself, Bella," said Fernando, tugging at the material.

Bella held the covers tight. "Please, allow me some privacy."

"Privacy?" asked Fernando. "Why?"

Bella could not answer. She just held the covers around her and stared blindly at the dresses.

"Get dressed," said Fernando, and left the room muttering to himself.

Bella swayed. She felt light-headed. She leaned on the wardrobe and took a few deep breaths, then reluctantly pulled out the first dress that was hanging on the rail. It was a white dress with floral patterns. To her dismay, it barely came to her knees. The other dresses were the same length.

"They are too small," she called out.

Fernando stepped into the room again, quicker than Bella had imagined, as if he'd been waiting. She wondered if he had been watching her through the gap in the door.

"I do not want to disappoint you," she said.

"What's wrong with it?" he asked. His hand automatically began to smooth Bella's hair behind her ear. "You look so pretty wearing it."

His wandering hands began to pull the dress up behind her, but she manoeuvred away.

"It is too short," she said. "Look." She gestured to her legs.

"My dear, Bella," Fernando began, "you have a lot of things to learn about Athens and Europe. You look beautiful, and I am sure that all the men will be looking at you when we are outside."

"But I do not want them to look at me."

Fernando sighed and checked his watch. "I think we have time for one quick lesson before we leave."

9

THE BEAST IS BACK

"So we have all this tech gear but no-one to operate it?" said Melody.

They were parked up in a maze of back streets away from the city centre.

"Just take what you need and what you can carry," said Derby. "The rest can all be picked up later."

"I wouldn't count on it still being here," said Melody, glancing over her shoulder at three homeless men sat on the steps of a rundown residential building behind them. They sat and watched Melody and the two men as they sorted through the gear.

"The laptops are encrypted, the v-Sat is useless without the network credentials, and we're taking the weapons," said Barnet. "So what? They'll get a bunch of stuff they can't use, and a van that the police are looking for in conjunction with a shooting in the city centre." He pulled his pack over his shoulder.

"Agreed," said Melody, and hoisted her own pack off the van's wooden floor.

"We could torch it," said Derby. "It would destroy the prints."

"It would also give the local police a range. They'd know we were here and probably slip the hobos over there a few euros. They'd tell them when, and that would give the police a radius."

Barnet began to walk off down the hill. The view of the sea above the houses added serenity to the otherwise tense morning.

"Barnet?" said Derby. "Where are you going?"

"You two can argue all you like about what we do with that piece of junk," he called back. "But I'm out of here. The clock is ticking."

"He's right," said Melody, collecting her peli-case with her Diemaco rifle held snugly inside in its foam inserts.

Derby slammed the van door shut and locked it. The two of them joined Barnet, who had continued to head down the hill with his head held firmly to the phone in his hand.

"So what do we have?" asked Melody. "I have my Diemaco. I can find myself a perch and cover you two if you want to find a weakness in that old fence?"

"I have my Sig, plus we both have MP-5s in our packs," said Derby. "There's a strip of wasteland between the boat-yard and the next one. I suggest Barnet and I take a side each. Can you cover us both?"

"Shouldn't be an issue in daylight," replied Melody.

"You have a perch in mind?"

"The apartment building," said Melody. "It's perfect."

"But what about-"

"Sharp?" asked Melody. "I'm sure he won't mind me. Besides, I'll be up on the roof."

"You don't think it's a bit close for comfort?"

"Derby, from up there I can shoot the first person who steps out of that workshop. If you two are inside the perimeter, you'll have free reign of the outside. But once you're on the inside, I'll lose all visual, and you'll be on your own. That MP-5 will be your only friend. Remember, priority one is to get Reg and Jess out, the second is to save the refugees. The only way we're going to accomplish that is by taking down Ferez and his men."

"One thing bothers me, Melody," said Derby. "If there were enough of them to take Reg, Jess and all the others, we're going to need to be pretty tight for three of us to get through them."

"I thought about that too," said Melody. "But Reg and Jess aren't exactly trained killers. It was only you, Barnet and me that were ever going to go tactical and take them down anyway."

"Like I said, Melody," said Derby. "If they took Gordon and Sharp down-"

"Then we'll just need to make sure it's us that comes out on top," said Melody. "We're the last line of defence here. Reg and the others will be depending on us."

"Okay, let's split up," said Barnet, who stood waiting on the corner of a small intersection in the backstreets. "Derby and I will take the flanks. Melody, if you get yourself up on the roof, we'll give you ten minutes to put your weapon together before we move in."

"Yep," agreed Melody. "It should be enough time to get set up. We don't have comms so do as much as you guys can in the open, and I'll pick them off as they appear."

"Got it," said Derby. "Right, move now. I'll mark ten minutes. Be ready."

———

Harvey studied the boatyard, committing the layout to memory, and then left the apartment building by the stairs.

He took the fire exit door that led to a warren of alleyways to the rear of the building, thinking that the front door would be monitored. The old fire escape looked as though it hadn't been used for years.

For Harvey's plan to work, his assumptions needed to be correct. He had no real facts. He didn't know who the men were, or how trained they would be.

Expect the worst.

Harvey's assumptions were based on stealth. If two men tried to enter the boatyard, they wouldn't walk through the gate; they'd use the wasteland to either side of the yard. And they'd split up. One team on the right side, one on the left, leaving a sniper somewhere to call the shots.

They'd go in on foot, and for that, they'd need to prep somewhere quiet before they stepped into the open, somewhere like the maze of backstreets in which Harvey now found himself.

If his assumptions were wrong, it would be a big mistake. He'd left the boatyard wide open.

Harvey turned a corner quietly. He saw the first man, crouched down in a doorway, rummaging through a backpack. He moved quickly but controlled.

Harvey took one step at a time, slow and silent, keeping out of the man's peripheral vision as much as he could. Only when Harvey got up close behind him, he saw the man was assembling an MP-5 from the parts in his pack, and that his Sig stuck out of his waistband.

"Don't move," said Harvey, quiet but firm. "Don't turn around."

The man froze.

Harvey whipped the Sig from the man's belt.

"Hands," said Harvey.

The man raised his hands.

Harvey checked the MP-5. It was still missing the bolt and magazine. No danger there.

"You have cuffs?"

"In my-"

"No talking," said Harvey. He kept three steps back. A trained man could spot an opportune moment to turn the tables.

"Cuff yourself," said Harvey. "Tight."

He waited and checked all around him as the man pulled a pack of plasticuffs from his bag, and began to put them on.

"Tight," Harvey reminded him.

The man gave a sharp jerk to demonstrate how tight they were.

"Okay, time for answers," Harvey began. "Where's the rest of the team?"

"Mate," said the man, turning his head.

Harvey slammed the butt of the handgun into his temple.

"I said, don't turn around."

The cuffed man knelt on the ground and winced at the pain. A small trickle of blood began to run from the fresh wound.

"Where's the rest of you?" asked Harvey.

"Rest of who?" the man replied.

"You don't know me. You don't know what I'm capable of. So I'll give you that one," said Harvey. "Any more lies or cheap attempts at stalling for time, and I'll cut your throat."

Harvey remained totally calm. The man had begun to sweat, a sure sign of fear. Adrenaline would be surging through him, and fight or flight would kick in. Harvey needed to control that. He needed the fear.

"Do I need to ask again?" he asked the man.

"I don't know. We split up."

"So what's the plan?" asked Harvey.

"What plan?"

"I warned you once."

The man sighed. "You don't know who you're dealing with here, mate."

"Can I presume judging by the fact that you're on the north side of the boatyard that your mate is somewhere back there on the south side also assembling an MP-5?"

The man didn't reply.

"I'll be honest with you," said Harvey. "In four and a half hours, I'll be dragging your body into that boatyard along with your friend's. I can kill you fast or slow, and that all depends on what you tell me."

Harvey felt the man's body relax, a sign of defeat. His next reaction would determine Harvey's. He would either break down, deny knowledge and beg, or he'd be aggressive.

"Go fuck yourself," said the man.

Harvey smiled and raised the gun to the back of his head.

An approaching car caught Harvey's attention. He kicked the man forward through the open doorway into the abandoned shop. Harvey followed him inside then helped him to his feet by pulling on the back of his shirt.

"Up," said Harvey, shoving him towards the staircase. Harvey looked around. The room was a mess with smashed furniture across the floor and the door hanging off its hinges.

"To the top," said Harvey, following at a safe distance.

"I'm telling you, mate. You don't know who you're dealing with here."

Harvey didn't reply.

At the top of the stairs, the man paused and turned back to Harvey.

"Do you really want to do this?" he asked.

Harvey kicked him through to the roof but noticed as he followed that the doors were riddled with bullet holes. He scanned the small roof space as his prisoner struggled to get to his feet.

"Talk to me," said Harvey. "Tell me what you're doing here."

"Same as you mate, earning a living," he replied. Harvey caught him searching the surrounding rooftops, probably for one of his team.

"Do you know who I am?"

"Why would I know you? Are you famous?"

"I try not to be," said Harvey. "Who do you work for?"

"I deliver pizza."

"With an MP-5?" Harvey began to circle the man. He stopped behind him.

"It's a rough neighbourhood," said the man, and started to turn.

"Face the front," said Harvey. "Don't move."

"Are you going to tell me who *you* work for?"

Harvey ignored him.

"What do you know about the girls?"

"*Girls?*"

"The refugees," said Harvey. "What do you know about them?"

"Not a lot. Did they order pizza?"

"You know what? I really didn't want to have to kill you, but you are beginning to piss me off."

"Am I supposed to be scared?"

Harvey was impressed. All too often, he came up against men that crumpled when they faced death. This man was behaving differently. It was something beyond training.

Harvey moved in. He placed the muzzle of the handgun into the base of the man's spine and searched his pockets for his wallet. He found it with his phone, a small folding case with some euros and an ID card.

"Your name's Barnet?"

"That's with a capital B."

Harvey saw the back of the man's ears lift as he grinned with sarcasm.

"Well, Barnet," said Harvey, tossing the wallet to the floor, "on your knees."

"I prefer to die standing up if it's all the same to you."

Harvey kicked out at the back of the man's legs. He immediately fell to the ground.

"Knees," said Harvey.

Barnet rolled over to his front and managed to shuffle onto his knees with his hands still bound tight by the plasticuffs.

"I prefer it when you kneel," said Harvey. "I get less blood on my clothes."

He raised the weapon once more to Barnet's head and saw the defiant man squeeze his eyes shut. It was make or break time. Harvey had seen even the toughest men break just moments before they were about to die. Harvey paused just long enough to give Barnet that chance.

It was during that decisive few seconds when his life hung in the balance of Harvey's intuition that Barnet's phone began to vibrate.

———

"You look pretty in that dress," said Fernando, as he pulled the car away from his house. He reached across and put his hand on Bella's exposed thigh. She shuddered at his touch.

"It won't always be like this," he said, removing his hand. "One day soon, you will be more willing. It will be easier."

Bella stared out of the window, seeing Athens for the first time in daylight.

"What do you think of my city?" asked Fernando.

"I haven't seen much of it," she replied.

"But from what you see now, it's pretty, no?"

"The flowers are colourful."

"And look at the ocean, Bella." Fernando held his hand out in front, presenting her with the Mediterranean. "See how it sparkles like thousands of jewels. It has always captivated me."

"Captivated?" asked Bella. "What is this?"

"It is when a person is so fixed on something, they cannot bear to turn their head and look elsewhere."

"And what is the opposite of captivated?" asked Bella. She remained watching the houses pass by, but she wasn't really looking.

"It is repulsed," said Fernando.

"Repulsed?"

"Repulsed."

"So if a person cannot bear to look at something, they are repulsed?"

"Yes."

"And if they cannot bear to turn away, they are captivated?"

"Yes," said Fernando. "Where did you learn English? It is very good, I have to say."

"My father was strict. He made me learn," began Bella. "He said that one day I would use English more than my own language."

"He's a smart man," replied Fernando. "Is he-"

"He's dead," snapped Bella. "Can we leave it there?"

"Yes," said Fernando. "Yes, we can. I'm sorry. I just want to know you, Bella. I want to learn you and hear about your past."

Bella bit her lip and fought back the tears, but her throat choked, and she gasped then sucked in a deep lungful of air.

"Bella?"

"You raped me, Fernando," she said, her voice thick with emotion. "You raped me in Syria, you raped me in Turkey, you raped me on the boats, and now you rape me in your home. But still, Fernando, still you tell me you care. You say that I'm pretty and that you want to know me, and want me to be happy." She dabbed at her eyes with the back of her hand, and Fernando passed her his handkerchief.

"I can't do this," she continued. "I cannot lie to myself. I cannot do the..." She struggled with the words. "Disgusting things you want me to do. You *repulse* me, Fernando. I cannot bear to look at you. So tell me how I'm supposed to marry you. How am I supposed to wait patiently at home all day with your children, and smile when you come home? How am I supposed to raise children when I am not happy? Our children will be unhappy. I just don't know-"

"Have you finished?" said Fernando, his tone bored as if he was tired of her whining. He pulled the car to the side of the road, cracked the window open for some fresh air, and pulled the handbrake up.

"Listen to me," he began. "I took you away from Syria. I saved your sorry little life."

"I paid you."

"You ungrateful bitch. I took you in good faith. You think four thousand dollars even comes close to what it costs? Wake up, Bella."

"It was everything we had."

"And I took it in good spirit."

"You took it because I was pretty, you told me."

"And I stand by that. I was..." Fernando searched for the word. "Captivated. I was captivated, Bella."

"And what about the others? You weren't so captivated by them, were you? I didn't see you giving them any special treatment, no wandering hands."

"I knew I wanted you, Bella," said Fernando, "from the first day I saw you, and you told me you wanted to run. I knew I could help, I knew it was my chance, and I prayed that nobody offered you a cheaper ride."

"You took all we had."

"I had to take something, Bella. It is a business. What am I supposed to say to my partner?"

"You mean your boss?"

"He's not my boss. We are partners."

"But he pays for everything, while you take all the risk?"

"We have an agreement," said Fernando.

"It doesn't matter anyway. You raped me. I can't even remember how many times now." The tears came back and Bella fought to suck air in between her loud sobs. "How can you say you care when you did that to me? You hurt me."

"But Bella, you have to understand," said Fernando. "Being on that boat with you after so long, seeing you every day, with those big brown eyes." He lowered his head. "I am ashamed, Bella. Forgive me."

"But in Syria, in the truck, it was the first time."

"I was captivated, Bella."

"It was my first time, Fernando," spat Bella under her breath. "Do you even know what that means?"

There was a silence. Bella rested her head on the cool glass and closed her eyes.

"The baby?" said Fernando, his voice soft with understanding. "The baby is mine?"

Bella nodded.

"We have a baby?" said Fernando. "Oh Bella, this is wonderful."

"The baby is the devil," she spat. "How can I bear a child that was born of rape? How can I love a child that-"

"But I can make this right, Bella," said Fernando, his voice pleading. "We can make it work. We can go to the shops and get the things you need. Let me show you, Bella."

Bella shook her head. She let the tears roll across her face without wiping her eyes.

"We can do this, Bella," said Fernando. He took her hand in her both of his then held it to his mouth and kissed it softly. "We can do this."

His manipulative words span around in Bella's head. It was like he had two faces, two minds. When he was soft, he could truly be gentle, but when the dark side appeared, he could be so cruel.

She opened her mouth to reply, but suddenly the windscreen shattered in their faces, and the roof of the car collapsed with a deafening bang.

Bella screamed and fought with the door handle as the body of a man in black slid slowly down onto the bonnet and stared at her with a deathly gaze.

10

TWO FACE

MELODY CROUCHED WITH HER BACK TO THE PARAPET WALL. She was on the rooftop of the old apartment building where they'd found Sharp's body. She moved fast. Flipping the lid of the peli-case open, she quickly pieced together her rifle. She could do it blindfolded and had done several times, both in her training and as part of her ongoing practice.

A loud thud broke the silence, followed by shattered glass raining down onto the concrete below. Melody finished attaching her scope before she stood and peered over the side. An old silver Mercedes roared away with a body on its bonnet. The driver didn't let off the accelerator as he swerved the car onto the main road, and the body of the man slid off onto the street. Melody crouched low and brought her rifle up to see through the scope.

It was Barnet.

"Shit."

The car tyres squealed again, and Melody moved the rifle in time to see the old Mercedes mount the pavement and burst through the gates to the boatyard. The car screeched to a halt outside what looked like a workshop building.

In all the chaos, movement caught her peripheral vision, and she just saw what looked like Derby diving for cover in the wasteland to the south side. She scanned the narrow strip of sand and trees for movement then moved across to the boatyard.

Everything happened so fast. Melody couldn't find the driver in her scope, but he'd left the door open. There was no movement. It had been a few seconds of chaos, then nothing.

She moved the rifle in horizontal layers across the huge expanse of the boatyard, stopping at each salvage boat before marking them as clear and moving on. It was her methodical way of clearing an area. The wasteland to the north was empty as far as she could see.

They were down to two now, just Derby and her, and the only protection Derby had was Melody. She suddenly realised how vulnerable she was on the roof. There would be no escape if somebody burst onto the rooftop, and by the time she swung the long Diemaco around, she'd be dead.

Melody reached for her Sig in her waistband and placed it on the parapet wall. Then, as an extra precaution, she wedged the door shut with a heavy coping tile that had fallen from the parapet wall. It wouldn't stop anyone for long, but maybe long enough for her to get the upper hand.

Melody returned to the wall and swung the rifle to the south side wasteland. She knew Derby would be low, looking for a weak spot in the perimeter fence.

She just had a few minutes, and then Derby would be inside and making his way to the workshop. But he'd still be expecting Barnet to come in from the far side. She scanned the boatyard again just as the door to the workshop was kicked open.

A man appeared at the door, peering around cautiously.

It was Fernando Ferez.

Melody had him in her sights. He lit a cigarette. Melody

calmed her breathing. Her finger touched the trigger.

Fernando had seen Derby. Melody could see him peering between the boats.

She breathed in once.

He was calling to Derby.

Melody exhaled. She waited until the very end of her breath then squeezed the trigger.

But Ferez had ducked inside, and the round found the concrete in a puff of dust. Melody moved the rifle across to Derby's position.

"Yes," she said when she saw Derby had broken through the fence and was making his way towards the workshop. "One hundred and fifty meters, Derby. You can do this."

Derby got himself within range of the workshop and crouched down, brought his MP-5 up on its sling, and tucked his Sig into his waistband.

"Come on, Derby."

Melody moved her weapon and focused on the door to the workshop.

"Come on, you bastard, show yourself."

Time seemed to stand still.

She moved back to Derby. He'd repositioned by the side of a boat to give himself a clearer view of the workshop door.

Melody wished they had comms but it had been too risky to use since the initial abductions. She swung the Diemaco back to the workshop for a moment, then returned to Derby to see a figure in black step up behind him and drag him out of sight behind a boat.

"*No*." She almost screamed aloud. "Shit, shit, shit."

The workshop door was kicked open again with a crash. Melody kept her rifle on Derby's position but turned her head to see Ferez running from the workshop using two hostages as cover.

It was Reg and Jess.

"What's happening?" Melody whispered.

Melody looked back through the scope to find Derby. It looked like a fight was taking place behind the boats. The two men rolled on the ground with the MP-5 between them. Derby's head appeared just briefly, and Melody moved her finger away from the trigger as soon as she saw him.

"Keep your cool, girl," she told herself.

Then the fight came to an abrupt halt, and the man in black stood over Derby's unmoving body.

"What the...?"

The man in black then moved towards the workshop.

"Come on, one more step and you're mine."

He stepped into view, edging slowly along the side of the boat.

"I've got you now."

Melody's finger found the trigger. She relaxed her breathing, felt the wind, and adjusted half a click on her scope as the man emerged.

She began to squeeze the trigger then felt the familiar thump of the rifle's kickback into her shoulder. Reloading quickly and collecting the spent round, Melody watched the mystery man tumble away and hit the ground as if some invisible force had hit him.

"Gotcha."

Melody's spirits lifted; the tables were turning. She refocused on the man, hoping for the kill shot. But neither he nor Derby were anywhere to be seen.

"Where have you gone?"

She scanned the boatyard once more.

Was Derby alive?

If he was, now they had a fighting chance. Then things took a turn for the worse.

"Give me a break."

Fernando had led Reg and Jess to a waiting boat at

gunpoint. He cowered behind Reg. Again, Melody had no clear shot. He shoved Jess onto the deck, followed by Reg, who stumbled and fell onto her.

Fernando quickly untied the bowline and threw the rope onto the front of the boat. He then stepped off the dock, suddenly in clear view. Melody fired. But it had happened too fast. She'd rushed. The shot went wide and careened off the boat's bimini frame.

Fernando realised he was being shot at and ducked out of view behind the boat's central controls. He fired up the two big on-board engines and immediately pulled the throttles into reverse.

Derby suddenly came into the view of her scope. He'd run from between the boats with one bloodied hand on the back of his head, waving his other arm at the boat.

What was he doing?

Melody's heart was racing. She felt useless from her perch. Too many obstructions had blocked any chance of her getting a clean shot.

Then, just as Fernando was making his escape with Reg and Jess, the man in black staggered out behind Derby carrying his MP-5. The shot was clear as day with no obstructions.

Melody lowered her head, slowed her breathing, and at the peak of her exhale, she began to squeeze the trigger.

The man turned and stared directly up at Melody as if he'd felt himself in her sights. His white t-shirt was stained red across the right-hand side, and though he clutched his shoulder, clearly pained, he stood tall and fearless, cradling Derby's MP-5.

She knew that look too well.

"Harvey?"

Only when Harvey had slammed the man's face into the hard concrete, felt his body fall limp and then rolled him onto his back, did he see whom he'd been fighting. Harvey had met him just briefly the previous month in London. He worked with Melody and Reg. He was one of the new guys that had joined the team in a small bar for end of week drinks. Suddenly, it all made sense.

He was Barnet's partner.

It wasn't a rival gang trying to stop Ferez; it was the British Government. More accurately, the guy was one of Melody's team. Or at least, he was posing as one of the team.

Which meant that Melody would be out there somewhere, and she'd be alone.

"Derby?" he said. "Wake up."

Harvey slapped him.

Derby was alive, but his head was bleeding, and he was out cold. Harvey checked around him, but the cannibalised boats on the trailers surrounding his position blocked his view of the workshop.

Harvey took Derby's MP-5 and stood with his back to the side of the old Bayliner. He edged along slowly to get a view of the workshop. But then, like the silence before a car crash, he felt a pang of voyeurism; he was being observed.

The feeling lasted just a fraction of a second before something red-hot slammed into his shoulder with the force of a hammer. He stumbled and fell over Derby. Immediately, he felt the warm trickle of blood soak his shirt and cling to his skin. It had been a clean shot, in and out. Another inch to the side and it would have missed entirely. Harvey lay for a few seconds, clutching his wound, stemming the flow of blood.

He lay dazed on the ground and felt Derby stand behind him. He heard his boots walking away groggily across the concrete.

"Derby," he called out.

But he hadn't heard.

Harvey got his knees and forced himself to his feet, then staggered behind Derby, who was running towards the boat that Ferez was using to escape. Harvey followed behind him, running out into the open. He painfully raised the weapon.

He heard the unmistakable sound of a bullet ricocheting off metal. An image of the apartment flashed through his mind. It was the perfect building for a sniper.

And he knew the perfect sniper for the job.

He turned to face her. A tiny glint of light on the rooftop was her only tell-tale.

Harvey held his arms out as far as his damaged shoulder would allow, enough to show her it was him. He knew he'd be in her sights, and he knew he had seconds before she pulled the trigger. He smiled up at her, hoping she would recognise him through her scope.

But then the flash of a muzzle told him otherwise.

The clatter of Derby's Sig scraping across the ground caused Harvey to spin and find Derby doubled over, clutching his hand in agony.

Harvey raised the MP-5 with his good arm.

"On your knees," said Harvey.

The man looked back

"Harvey?"

"Knees."

"Harvey, you remember me? I work with Melody. We met last month." Derby began to straighten.

Harvey set the selector to single shot and fired a single round into Derby's right foot, sending the man to the ground.

Derby screamed in agony. "What are you doing, you madman? I'm on your side."

"Is that right?" said Harvey.

"Of course I bloody am. I work with Melody." Derby pulled his boot off, wincing at the pain, and revealed a blood-soaked sock, inside which, Harvey could see there was a lot of damage. "Don't just bleeding stand there," said Derby, holding out his hand. "Help me up."

"You want a hand up?" asked Harvey.

"Don't mess about, mate," said Derby, breathless. "I'm in a lot of pain here."

"I can see."

"You know what? I liked you," began Derby. "Even when the guys at work told me stories about what you've done, I defended you. They spoke like you were some kind of monster, a law unto yourself, and unstoppable."

Harvey stared at him.

"They said you were crazy, and that most people are too afraid to even look at you," said Derby. "And when I asked them what you'd done and why you were like that, they just said that some people are born bad. It's in their blood."

Silence.

"You had a sister, right?"

Harvey didn't reply.

"She killed herself, didn't she?" Derby smiled. "It don't surprise me with a brother like-"

Quick as a flash, Harvey slammed the butt of the rifle into Derby's jaw. The large man fell back to the floor, his boot dropped to the ground by his side.

Harvey set to work.

He dragged Derby to the gantry, bound his hands with an off-cut of rope he found on one of the nearby boats, and hooked a chain around his neck. Then Harvey began to take up the slack with the chain hoist.

He glanced out to sea, but all that was left of Ferez's boat was the dissipating wake. With each pull, Derby raised a little further off the ground. His ruined foot dragged a trail of blood across the concrete.

Derby's feet slowly raised into the air. The lack of airflow shook him from his daze as his body fought to survive.

"Harvey," he choked.

Harvey continued to raise the man into the air.

"Stop it."

The chain was tightening with Derby's weight. His voice had become barely a whisper.

"Who put you up to it?" asked Harvey. "Don't hold out on me, Derby, I found Barnet and his phone. He's been talking to Ferez."

Derby's eyes were wide with fright.

"You're setting us up, aren't you?" said Harvey. "Melody and me. This whole thing is about getting us both here together. Who's running the show?"

Derby's panicked breathing came in short, sharp bursts.

"You're dirty," said Harvey. "Admit it, and I'll finish it."

Derby just stared back. His eyes had begun to bulge.

Harvey planted the heel of his foot hard into Derby's gut, sending his body swinging freely on the chain.

"I said, admit it," shouted Harvey, enraged by the traitor.

Derby tried to talk.

"Louder," said Harvey.

Derby tried to move his head but the chain held him tight.

"Blink once if you're a traitor."

Derby blinked.

"Blink once if you were out to kill me."

Derby coughed a spray of blood into the air. He blinked once.

Harvey nodded and raised the weapon to Derby's head.

"Blink once if you were out to kill Melody."

Derby tried to talk.

"I said, blink once if you were out to kill Melody," shouted Harvey, and rammed Derby's groin with the butt of his rifle.

Derby's face was a bright red mess of tears and blood. He blinked once.

"Last question," said Harvey. "Blink once if the order came from MI6."

Derby raised a vague smile, coughed once, and was then still. Harvey took a deep breath and fired the weapon into Derby's head to make sure. He tossed the rifle to one side and heard footsteps behind him.

"I wondered when you'd come," said Harvey, as he emptied Derby's pockets.

"What are you doing here, Harvey?"

Harvey was silent, as he thought about the answer carefully. "My moral compass," he said. "I never could turn it off."

"Do you know who that was?"

Harvey remained facing Derby, but the voice came from behind him, and he knew that at least one weapon would be trained on him.

"Yeah I know who he was," said Harvey. "The question is, do *you*?"

"Of course I do. That's why I'm wondering why you shot him and hung him out to dry."

"You shot him first," said Harvey with a smile.

"I shot his gun from his hand. He was about to kill you."

"Is that right?" said Harvey. "So why did you shoot me?"

"I didn't know it was you. Why didn't you tell me you were coming?"

"I tried to tell you."

"But I was busy?"

"That's right, you were busy," said Harvey. "Still, doesn't matter now, does it?"

"It still matters, Harvey. He was an MI6 operative. There's no going back."

"And Barnet?" asked Harvey. "I take it there's no going back from that either?"

"That was you?"

"Of course."

"What have you done, Harvey?" said Melody, her eyes wide. "Even Jackson won't be able to get you out of this."

"They were dirty, Melody. Didn't you hear him? How long were you stood there?"

"Seconds."

"So you missed the important bit," said Harvey.

"So tell me what he said."

"It wasn't what he said, Melody," said Harvey. "It was what he didn't say."

———

Fernando gunned the engine and the car roared out of the side street onto the main beach road. The body slid off the car as he wrenched the steering wheel left. The tyres squealed as if they would rip off the wheels as he swung the car again and burst through the gates of his boatyard, smashing off their hinges and sending them crashing to the ground.

Fernando didn't let off the throttle once. He swerved between the boats and slammed on the brakes outside the workshop.

"Bella, I want you to get to the boat, get inside and stay out of sight."

"But, Fernando, I'm scared. What's happening?"

His phone had begun to vibrate and he hit the green button to answer the call. In the silence that followed the previous chaos and above the pounding drum of Bella's heart, she heard the man say a single sentence.

"One man down."

The call was disconnected.

"Just do as I say," said Fernando, clearly shaken. "I have something to deal with, and then I will join you."

Fernando pushed the door open and ran into the work-shop, leaving her in the car alone.

She sank down in her seat, afraid to move.

Shouting came from the workshop, but it wasn't Fernando's voice; it was an Englishman. Then Fernando kicked the door open and disappeared inside.

"What have I done?" she asked herself.

To her surprise, the tears didn't come. She felt them inside her, behind her eyes, but they refused to show. Instead, her breathing relaxed, and she sat calmly. Her world spun. Her mind was thick with regret, sorrow, loss, guilt. But still, the tears refused to come.

She had to get away. She had to find a moment to escape Fernando. But a part of her wanted to stay. A part of her felt an obligation to the other girls; maybe they were still escaping Syria, maybe they hadn't met Fernando yet, but Bella knew that more girls would cross his path in the days, weeks and months ahead.

"I can stop this," she thought. "It is my responsibility."

She had known a boy like Fernando at home when she had been a child, a boy called Azad. He'd walked God's world as if God himself had created it just for him, and as if every other man owed him something, like he was above everybody, even God.

But Bella knew that these people came crashing down sooner or later. Society doesn't tolerate people like that for long. Her community had grown tired of Azad's dealings. Too many children had complained to his parents, his father had dished out too many futile beatings, and one day, Azad had seriously hurt a young girl, so badly that she could never bear children. The fathers of the other children took it upon themselves to straighten the boy out, to teach him the way of God, of love and life.

Bella's father had been one of those men. He later spoke

to Bella on the subject. It was one of the few times he had sat her down to talk as a father might talk to his child. Her father hadn't said what the men had done to Azad, or what lessons they had taught him. She'd found that out for herself from her friends.

Bella had asked her father why they did not show Azad kindness, as is God's wish that evil be met with kindness. Her father had simply replied that a man that wields the fires of hell must earn kindness.

A few days had passed until Bella had spoken to her friend, whose father had not been so tight-lipped about the lessons. Although nobody in the village spoke of the incident publicly, it was clear that all the villagers knew what had happened. Even at school, her teacher hadn't acknowledged the vacant seat where Azad had sat. Azad had been one of the oldest in the mixed class. He had always called out, louder than the rest of the children. There was a void in his absence, but nobody complained.

Bella's friend had told her that the men had taken the boy to the top of the jebel, a full two day's hike away. They stripped him and burned his possessions, then dragged him naked over the sharp rocks so his ruined feet would always remind him of his return journey. They cut away the boy's eyelids so that he could forever see the damage he had caused. Finally, they tied the boy to a fig tree with bark as white as the hair on her grandfather's head, and cut all but two of his fingers off, one on each hand. For this, they told him he could count the choices he had: redemption or perpetual castigation, an outcast forever.

Azad had never returned, and life had resumed as close to normal as it could have.

Like Azad, Fernando would come crashing down.

Gunfire woke Bella from her daze. A bullet hit the concrete and sprayed a puff of dust into the air. Fernando was in front of her with a man and woman. They were running to the boat.

Bella reached for the door handle.

"Leave," she whispered, pleading to the empty car.

She heard the boat engine roar into life, and saw Fernando duck down as if someone was shooting at him, someone Bella could not see.

She sank lower in the car then looked across to the door Fernando had left open. If only she could close it and drive away. She heard the scuffle of feet, and another single gunshot close by.

Bella closed her eyes and considered running. But maybe she would be shot. She wondered if it was the man Fernando had spoken to, the dangerous man.

Am I safe now?

A few minutes passed. Bella watched Fernando making his escape on the boat. She revelled in the relief that washed over her.

A woman stepped from behind the workshop. She carried a large rifle, larger than the type her father had used for hunting.

Bella thought that she was pretty but tough. She stared at her white skin and dark features from the safety of the car. The woman looked perfect. She began to talk to someone behind the car; the dangerous man that Fernando had spoken to maybe?

All Bella heard was the mumbled murmurs, but the tension had eased. There was peace between these two people. Bella chanced a glance into the side mirror. She saw the back of the woman in her black clothes, and the back of the man. Blood ran freely from his shoulder. He'd been shot.

And a dead man hung from a big steel frame behind him.

LIVESTOCK

THE INSIDE OF THE WORKSHOP SMELLED OF COUNTLESS years of oil spills, sweat and cheap cigarettes. The only light shone through tiny cracks in the walls and roof, sending laser-like beams to the feet of the seventeen prisoners that stood at the edges of the room tied to hooks fixed high into the walls.

"Melody," cried Ladyluck. "Oh my God, it's you. Thank God." She began to sob in the dark.

"Are we all here?" asked Melody.

She looked around the room and saw in the shadows the frightened white eyes of nine more people.

"What the-?"

"Refugees," said Harvey. "Ready for the truck."

"Is anyone hurt?" asked Melody.

"Over here," came a voice from the corner of the room.

"Who's there? What's wrong?" asked Melody.

"It's my friend. They beat her, and..." Her voice broke. "Please help her. She's dying."

"Harvey, find a light or a lamp or something," said Melody. She made her way towards the voice.

Harvey rummaged through the unorganised tools on the

benches and systematically emptied the shelves of the metal cabinet that stood near the door. Eventually, he found what he was looking for. He clicked the switch for the battery-powered lamp, and a dim light suddenly illuminated the frightened faces of the prisoners. They turned their heads to protect their eyes.

Harvey took the lamp over to Melody and saw that the girl's torn clothes were soaked in blood from the waist down.

It was the girl from the last photo he'd received.

"I'll take care of her," said Melody, moving to protect the girl's modesty. "What's her name?"

"Alia," said the girl who had called to Melody. "Her name is Alia."

"Alia, can you hear me?" said Melody. She searched for signs of life and felt the warm but soft brush of the girl's body exhaling.

"Alia, I'm going to help you. Can you stand?"

A single tear ran from the girl's eye.

Melody checked her legs for breaks by running her hands from the feet upwards to the thighs, but the girl flinched when Melody reached the dried blood on her bare skin.

"It's okay. I'm not going to hurt you," said Melody. Alia's eyes followed Melody's hands with a lazy flicker of exhaustion. Melody pulled the lamp closer and searched for the source of the blood. She found barbed wire around the tops of Alia's thighs. The rusty barbs had torn her apart. Melody continued her examination, moving up to the girl's stomach. She felt ribs, far too pronounced, and beneath her dress, she found more barbed wire wrapped around Alia's chest beneath her arms.

Melody looked away. There was no need to expose the girl with so many onlookers.

"She was hung from it," said Harvey behind her. "The barbed wire. Ferez sent me a photo."

Melody reached out and smoothed the girl's hair. "Alia, listen, we're going to get you to a doctor, okay?"

She didn't respond.

Melody felt the faint pulse on Alia's wrist.

"You're going to be okay. Do you hear me?"

But as she said the words, shock and loss of blood overcame the girl's fragile body.

"No, no," said Melody, feeling for a pulse on her neck. "Help me," she called to Harvey.

But Harvey just placed his hand on her shoulder. "Melody-"

"Untie her," she said. "Get that wire off her."

"Melody, stop."

The room was silent. All eyes were on Melody.

"She's gone," said Harvey. He gave her shoulder a squeeze.

Melody let her head hang in defeat. Then she pulled on the girl's ruined clothes to keep her covered. "How long do we have?" she asked, refusing to remove her gaze from Alia's face.

"She's not hurting anymore, Melody," said Harvey.

He rubbed her shoulder and pulled her into him. But Melody was resolute. Her determine had been triggered. Harvey knew the look.

"Ferez was here a while ago. He took Reg and Jess," said Ladyluck.

"We saw him get away on his boat," spat Melody. "Coward."

"He called someone when he was here. He was frightened. Somebody called Streaky. He told him to bring the trucks now. I think they are moving the refugees early."

As if the driver was waiting for his cue, they heard the distant sound of a heavy diesel engine pulling into the boatyard.

"Quick," said Melody. "Help me untie them. We can save them."

"No," said Harvey. "There's no time." He moved to the door and watched as the truck drew closer, slowly manoeuvring through the array of boats and trailers.

"What do you mean, no?" replied Melody, reaching up to Ladyluck's bound arms.

"Leave them."

"Harvey?" said Melody. "Help me get them down. We can still rescue them."

"Do you trust me, Melody?"

"Of course I do. I-"

"I've got an idea."

———

Bella saw two trucks arriving in the car's side mirror. The man and woman were still in the workshop.

"This might be my last chance," she said to herself.

She slipped from the car to a space in the shadows between two boats. Then she climbed into one and pulled a heavy, oily tarp over her.

The squeal and loud hiss of the lorries' air brakes was followed by two engines shuddering to a noisy stop. Doors opened and slammed shut, and footsteps disappeared into the workshop.

Bella closed her eyes.

She wished for the thousandth time that she had just stayed in her village. She wished she hadn't travelled to Aleppo, and most of all, she wished she hadn't met Fernando. No matter how hard she tried, Bella couldn't put the image of her family being gunned down out of her mind. She tried to imagine herself there and indulged in a romantic thought of her and her family all holding hands. If they were to die, then they would die together.

The reality was that they'd never be given a chance to die as they wished. The stories that she'd heard of gunmen bursting into homes and just shooting anyone in sight in cold blood were more realistic.

Somebody screamed from inside the workshop. It wasn't a scream of pain, it sounded to Bella more like a scream of anger. Such cruelty, everywhere she went.

One by one, the refugees were led from the workshop to the second lorry. The scene played out before Bella's eyes. It was as if they were being led to the firing squad. It was just like the stories Bella had heard from Syria when the military had pulled entire families from their homes and slaughtered them on the streets. But the refugees would have a very different and more uncertain future.

Bella's chance of reaching England was slipping away. Perhaps it was gone forever now, for Bella at least. Uncertainty shrouded the faces of her people. Only fear guided them onto the truck.

The two men laughed and joked amongst themselves. One stood by the door to the workshop, counting the scared faces as they emerged from the darkness. The other stood at the back of the lorry, shoving the men up roughly and helping the two younger girls, rewarding himself with a grope of their chest as he did so.

From beneath the tarp, Bella could see directly into the cargo space of the truck. Large boxes stood to the sides with plastic sheeting draped across them. The refugees sat in a corner on the floor, just as Bella remembered them sitting on the floor of the cabin on the boat, huddled together for warmth and security.

It would be the last time Bella saw any of them. She tried to focus on their faces, to remember them. They would never meet again, but Bella thought she would think of them in the times to come and hope that they fared well.

More shouting emerged from the workshop. The cry was brief and female. The man who had stood at the rear of the truck had moved inside and out of sight, his movements lithe and slow.

He appeared at the door a few moments later with a well-dressed woman with blonde hair. She was not a refugee but was equally as scared. The woman's bare feet were bound and she shuffled painfully across the hard and rough concrete.

She never said a word. Even when she was assisted in boarding the truck and wandering hands ran up her skirt, she was silent. A look of disgust that twisted her face was the only sign she even felt the man's sly gropes. She sat alone with her knees drawn up and her head buried in her legs until the last hostage was led from the workshop.

It was the lady in black, the pretty one with pale skin and dark features. Her wrists were also bound, and like the first woman, she was treated to the same inquisitive hands as she climbed onto the flatbed of the truck. But this woman was different. She immediately returned her leg to the ground, turned, and in an instant, landed her forehead onto his nose.

Bella smiled from the safety of her hiding place.

Outraged, the man repaid the assault with a hard slap, and forced the woman onto the truck while holding his bloodied nose with one hand.

He spoke to her. Bella couldn't hear the words, but some things do not need to be heard; there was enough in the way he spoke.

The shutter door of the first truck was pulled shut and locked with a padlock, trapping the two woman inside. Bella wondered where they would be going. Not England. If they were going to England, they would surely be with the refugees.

The two men then moved to the back of the refugee truck. Bella tried to see the faces of the refugees for one last desperate attempt at contact with them, but they had all huddled too close together and averted their eyes from the two men outside. A few blankets were tossed inside and the man with the bloodied nose began to walk away.

To Bella's horror, he walked directly towards where she lay. She slowly lowered her head and pulled the tarp over her.

His footsteps were slow as if he had all the time in the world.

Then he stopped.

Bella dared not move. He was just a few feet away. She closed her eyes, just waiting for the tarp to be ripped back at any moment. But the moments grew longer. Was he watching her? She feared to make the slightest movement in case the tarp she was lying beneath made a sound and gave her away. Her breathing quickened. No matter how hard she tried to control it, her short breaths seemed so loud.

A trickle of liquid splashing onto the dry concrete was followed with a soft groan of pleasure. Was he urinating? Then he hacked up phlegm from deep inside him, a noise that Bella had hated even when her father had done the same.

The noise stopped.

"Fernando, where are you? We must leave if we are to make the border."

He was using the phone. Bella's heart sank when she thought of Fernando. He had escaped with two people, a man and a woman, but she prayed he wouldn't return. She doubted he would ever find her in the boat beneath the tarp. But Bella knew that a small twist of fate could align their paths once more, and her chances of escaping would be gone forever.

Bella was torn. Part of her wanted Fernando to return, to give her the chance of finishing him somehow. But she could never do it. Part of Bella wanted the men to drive the refugees away, to leave the boatyard so she could escape. But she didn't know where she would go. The most significant part of her wanted to end it all, for death to be on her terms.

"No, it's fine. It looks like there has been a war, but there's no-one else here, just the refugees, two hostages and a dead guy hanging from the gantry." He paused. "You left them on the island? Is it safe?"

Bella gasped, louder than she expected.

Another silence followed. Surely, he had heard. Bella's heartbeat on the boat's wooden floor pounded like a drum.

"Hold on, Fernando," said the man into the phone. "I thought I heard something."

Bella glanced up at the refugees inside the lorry and caught the eye of the young girl with whom she had once spoken. Her eyes widened with recognition. But Bella gave a soft shake of her head, pleading with her eyes for her to stay silent.

Time stood still.

The boat rocked slightly as he pulled himself up onto the trailer. Bella prayed that her feet could not be seen sticking out of the tarp. She prayed her breathing was not too loud.

"Ah, it's nothing," said the man, and jumped back to the ground.

Bella's gave a long quiet exhale. Her heart was thumping.

"The two women? We'll deal with them. I will do it personally. I will throw them from the cliffs. By the time their bodies are found, they will be unrecognisable."

The two women would be killed. Bella was sad for them. The second lady had been so strong with spirit.

"I'd say we need to clear out of this place, Fernando. Once we're gone, come and take what you need. We'll need to find someplace new to run the operation."

There was a silence while Fernando spoke to the man.

Bella pictured his huge ugly nose and two-sided voice. Was he angry or was he gentle when he spoke to his men?

"No, I haven't seen your little plaything." He laughed a cruel sneer. "She has probably gone and joined the homeless on the streets of Athens by now. She'll earn her keep; she was pretty."

Bella realised they were discussing her.

Fernando has noticed I am missing?

"Don't worry. If we see her, we'll kill her."

———

The last refugee was led from the workshop, leaving Melody and Ladyluck alone in the semi-darkness.

"This isn't good, Ladyluck," said Melody. "I've got a bad feeling here."

Ladyluck raised her head. She was clearly exhausted from standing and hanging with her arms in the air.

"Why? Do you want to go with *them*?" she replied.

"If we were put with the *refugees*, we could have helped them escape on the way to the UK," whispered Melody. "If we're being kept here, it means they have other plans for us."

"Like what?" asked Ladyluck, loud and excited. "What other plans would they have?"

Melody shot her a glance to shut her up.

"Don't look at me like that, Mills. Your boyfriend got you into this. If you hadn't listened to him, we'd both be outside right now."

"I'm sure Harvey has a plan," said Melody, more to herself than to Ladyluck.

The light from the door fell into shadow, and one of the men moved into the workshop. He walked slowly like a predator, eying them both.

"See anything you like?" asked Melody.

He smiled back then returned his attention to Ladyluck, stepping closer to her.

"Don't you dare touch me," warned Ladyluck. Her eyes narrowed to slits and her mouth looked as though it was ready to bite. The defensive reaction from Ladyluck surprised Melody. Although Ladyluck liked to appear in charge and the focus of attention, almost as an alpha-female, she wasn't hardy enough for ground operations.

The man laughed and reached out with his hand, resting one finger on Ladyluck's throat.

"Feisty," he said with a smile.

"Pig," replied Ladyluck.

He ignored the comment and continued to stare at his finger then slowly let it slide from Ladyluck's neck down her chest. He stopped momentarily. Melody could see the rise and fall of Ladyluck's chest.

A deathly silence filled the room. Melody wondered how she would react if his hand ventured to the right or left. The man stared at Ladyluck with lust, his grin spreading.

Ladyluck stared back, almost daring him to go further.

"Streaky, what are you doing?" came the other man's voice from the doorway.

Streaky winked at Ladyluck and removed his hand.

"Just a bit of window shopping, Jimmy," he replied.

"Load the truck, Streaky," said Jimmy. He continued to watch his partner with suspicion, as though his wandering hands were a common occurrence.

Streaky reached up and unhooked Ladyluck's bindings from the meat hook that hung from the ceiling. Relief washed over her face when her arms lowered. But Streaky ruined her small moment of pleasure by whispering in her ear loud enough for Melody to hear.

"There'll be plenty of time later, girls."

Melody studied Streaky's face. He wasn't a pleasant

looking man. His eyes were small and too close together, his skin was rough as if he'd spent his life at sea or in the open air, and the hair on his back and chest met his unshaven face with very little demarcation.

"Ladies first," said Streaky, presenting the way out to Ladyluck. He turned and winked at Melody. "You sit tight there, my lovely. I'll be back for you shortly."

"Can't wait," replied Melody, returning his stare.

Ladyluck shuffled out with her ankles bound but turned to Melody briefly before she was nudged through the doorway with Streaky's hand on her backside. Melody was alone finally. She wished she had listened to Harvey when he'd wanted to tie a fake knot so she could slip her hands in and out. But it had seemed too risky, and Melody had told him to tie the knot tight.

Melody focused on acting submissive. If Streaky wanted to play, she would tolerate him as much as she could. The last thing she wanted was for him to get rough and find the Sig tucked in the back of her waistband, or the knife strapped to her ankle.

Streaky stepped back in the room as if he was expecting her to be up to something. "There you are," he said, and seemed to slide into the workshop, side-stepping in front of Melody as a hunter might circle its prey.

"Where else would I be?" said Melody.

He disappeared from view behind her but made no sound. The only sign he was close was the stale smell of body odour that overpowered the oil and cigarettes ingrained into the walls.

"Are you going to be trouble?" he hissed, his mouth suddenly close to Melody's ear.

She closed her eyes and prepared for the worst.

"No," she said. "I don't want any trouble."

His hands landed on Melody's hips with an oddly gentle touch. He was dangerously close to finding the gun.

"You just wait until we're alone," whispered Streaky. His hands edged to her stomach and pulled her backwards. Melody grimaced at the feeling of his growing excitement.

"Streaky," called Jimmy from outside. "Are you going to load her up or what?"

Streaky took a final sniff of Melody's hair and ran his hands up her sides then her arms, where he unhooked her.

"No trouble, remember?" whispered Streaky. The feigned seductive tones had gone from his voice.

He nudged Melody forward. Harvey hadn't tied Melody's feet; there hadn't been time. So she walked slowly and calmly, and stopped at the back of the truck. Streaky was clearly too engrossed in thoughts of his later plans to notice.

Ladyluck was sat near the bulkhead behind the cab with her bound wrists over legs. She peered over her knees as Melody swung her leg onto the truck.

Streaky's hand found her backside, his fingers close to Melody's weapon. She immediately dropped her leg back down, span, and planted her forehead into his nose.

Streaky folded in half, clutching his face, and Melody started to climb up onto the truck as if nothing had happened. But before she could stand, Streaky landed his open palm against Melody's face. The blow stung, but Melody took it well; she didn't retaliate. If he found the gun, her chances of escape would be over.

Ladyluck looked on in awe and Melody dropped to sit in the opposite corner. The shutter door was pulled down with a crash, leaving them alone in the darkness.

"Hey, Ladyluck?"

There was a short silence followed by her scared and shaky voice. "Yes?"

"You remember when I told you I had a bad feeling?"

12

ROCKY MOUNTAIN PASS

Standing in the shadow of a tree, the roots of which had punched through the concrete, and an old wooden fishing boat sat dormant on a trailer, Harvey looked on with pride. Melody had handled herself well. But the problem remained that she and Ladyluck hadn't been loaded into the same lorry as the refugees. They were in a truck by themselves.

Harvey began to formulate a new plan.

He *could* walk out into the open and hope that the two men didn't have guns. But that was unlikely. The chances were they'd both be armed to the teeth, and if they didn't kill him, they'd shoot a refugee, or worse, Melody. He could wait to see if the trucks left the boatyard together in convoy. Either way, his chances of rescuing Reg and Jess were growing slimmer. Melody was armed, and he had to trust that she could handle herself.

One of the men began to walk towards Harvey's position. Harvey took three slow steps backwards until his back was up against the tree. He looked out of the shadows, ready to strike if need be.

It was the one called Streaky, the guy that Melody had hit. Harvey had heard his name being called. Streaky stopped on the other side of the boat to relieve himself.

Now would be the perfect time, thought Harvey. But acting on an impulse would be hasty. He needed a plan, but at the forefront of his mind, he knew that time was running out and his window of opportunity was fading away.

Scenarios played out in Harvey's mind, each vital detail seemed to be highlighted, as well as each risk. Many plans fell by the wayside as the risk increased and the odds of saving Reg and Jess grew higher. Another plan seemed reasonable, but the risk of Fernando escaping was too high. His plan needed to save the refugees, save Reg and Jess, and save Melody.

Streaky began to talk to Fernando on his phone.

"I will do it personally. I will throw them from the cliffs. By the time their bodies are found, they will be unrecognisable."

Streaky zipped up and walked away, still talking to Fernando. Harvey stepped out from the shadows. The engine of the first truck started. The man called Jimmy was at the wheel and lit a cigarette to begin his long journey.

Streaky finished his call and spoke with Jimmy, but the conversation was muffled over the sound of the diesel engine. Harvey crept around the back of the boats. While Streaky's back was turned talking to Jimmy, Harvey darted the twenty yards and stopped behind the refugee truck. He dropped and checked their feet.

He hadn't been seen.

Harvey was counting on Jimmy leaving with the refugees, so he'd be left alone with Streaky. Jimmy slammed his door shut. Things were moving. Harvey crouched beneath the lorry and watched as Streaky took a lazy stroll to his vehicle, which had Melody and Ladyluck inside.

Jimmy began to rev the engine.

Harvey rolled his neck to the left, waited for the click, and then to the right.

He was ready.

But then, Streaky also started his engine, and the driver's door slammed. Harvey peered beneath the refugee lorry and saw Melody's truck begin to roll away. He dropped to the ground, rolled beneath the vehicle and pulled himself up, just as Streaky rolled past.

Harvey could do nothing except watch as Melody was driven out of the boatyard and headed north away from the city, along the coastal mountain road.

———

"Hold your hands out," said Melody in the semi-darkness. She reached for the knife strapped to her ankle.

"What? Why?" said Ladyluck, her voice thick with tears.

"Have you been crying, Ladyluck?"

"We're going to die, you heard them," said Ladyluck. "I'm not ready to die. Oh, why did I come here?"

"Pull yourself together," snapped Melody. "You're not dead yet, and all the time I'm here, you're not going to die."

Ladyluck was silent, except for a sniff. She wiped her eyes with her bound hands.

"Hold your hands out, Ladyluck."

Melody felt for her wrists and began to slice through the rope.

"You have a knife?" said Ladyluck. "But I don't see what good it will do. Didn't you see him? He had a gun."

"Yeah well, you make your own luck in life, and I'm not going down without a fight," said Melody. "Now take the knife and cut my wrists free."

Ladyluck did as she was told, fumbling in the dark. She then returned the knife to Melody.

"Right," said Melody. "Now to get us out of here."

"I heard him padlock the shutter," said Ladyluck. "We'll never get it open."

"Never say never," said Melody, running her hands across the shutter. It comprised of five-inch horizontal slats that were hinged together, which allowed the door to roll up and over along the steel rails.

Melody searched in the dark and found a screw head. She tested it with the point of her knife then felt the satisfying click of the screw unfastening.

A few moments later, she dropped it to the floor and smiled in the dim light at Ladyluck. "We're in business."

Just then, the lorry took a sharp turn and hit an incline. Streaky must have dropped down a gear to take a hill, and the two women were thrown to the floor.

"He's climbing a hill. We must be close to the cliffs," said Ladyluck.

Melody rolled off her and immediately got to work on the remaining screws.

"What are you planning, Melody?" asked Ladyluck. "You're not going to jump from a moving truck, are you?"

Melody tossed another screw to the floor and then moved to the other side.

"Whatever happens, Ladyluck," she replied, "you can be sure I'm not going anywhere without you."

————

Harvey was thankful when the refugee truck turned left out of the boatyard and took the same road as Melody. But the first truck was already out of sight.

The harsh concrete rushed passed just two feet below

Harvey. His feet were hooked over a strut. He clung with his arms to the spare tyre, using all of his core strength to keep his torso from dropping and scraping along the road surface.

The rear bumper, a single beam of steel that looked more like a step than a bumper, was designed to prevent smaller cars from being wedged below the lorry's undercarriage in the event of a crash; it was two feet away from where he hung.

Harvey reached out with his left leg and hooked his foot over the beam. The move stretched his body out and increased the pull on his stomach. His shoulders began to shake with the strain. He took a few deep breaths, and in one smooth motion, moved his right foot to join the left on the steel beam. His two feet stuck out from the rear of the moving lorry.

Then, using the momentum from the move, he swung one arm across to the rear beam. Suddenly, the lorry took a turn. It hit a hill. Streaky crunched down a gear, creating a considerable jolt throughout the lorry.

Harvey's right hand slipped off the spare wheel and swung dangerously close to the road below. His balance was off. But he used the swing to make the final move to the beam and clung to it with all his remaining strength.

The lorry was still climbing. It had slowed enough for Harvey to pull himself straight and stand up, holding onto the padlock with one hand and searching for a handhold on the smooth rear shutter of the truck with the other.

The vehicle crested a hill and began to cruise down a short stretch of road. Harvey used the opportunity to edge to the corner and peer in front. There was a space between the truck's body and the loose shutter; it was just wide enough for Harvey to slot his fingers inside.

To one side, tall cliffs whizzed past, and to the other, the world dropped out of sight over the cliffs.

Harvey reached up, sliding his hands inside the gap, and

then placed his left boot against the smooth shutter door, ready to climb to the roof. He peered around the edge once more, just as the lorry reached the trough and began another uphill climb. He'd need to wait until a downward stretch to give him as much chance as possible of scaling the truck.

One of the wheels found a pothole, which sent a violent jolt through to Harvey's precarious position. His right boot lost its grip on the beam and Harvey fell, somehow managing to keep his fingers inside the sharp groove. But his boots slid and bounced on the road, wrenching his body backwards.

Harvey's body stretched out and twisted painfully. He couldn't even let go; the pull on his fingers had wedged his fingers tight. They slowed as they crested another small hill then began to pick up speed. Harvey's boots were quickly grinding away and getting hot.

Harvey clenched his teeth, took three deep breaths, his fingers burning with pain, and dragged his left foot closer to the truck, his right continued to drag along the road.

The moment his left foot hooked over the beam, he gave one final pull and dragged his right foot up out of danger then sat on the narrow steel beam while his boots cooled down. Harvey's feet were burning. The soles of his shoes had begun to melt. His fingers screamed in agony; they were wedged deep and uncomfortably into the sharp groove.

With a final push, he stood up against the flat back of the truck once more. He pulled his fingers from the gap, flexed them, and then pushed them back in, as deep as they would go, gripping onto almost nothing but sharp steel and fibreglass.

Harvey placed his foot against the back of the shutter and without hesitation, he pulled himself up, pushing against the truck with his leg and sliding his fingers deeper into the gap. Then he pushed with his other leg until he could see over the roof. One more agonising push with all his might and his hand reached over onto the smooth fibre-glass roof of the truck. Harvey swung his leg and pulled his whole body up. He lay for a moment to let his fingers regain some blood.

But the break was a mistake.

A sharp right turn immediately sent him into a slide towards the edge. He slammed his boot down, trying to gain friction. The lorry entered a steep incline, which threatened to throw him off the back. Harvey forced his other boot down. But he still moved slowly. He was in an even worse position than before.

Seconds felt like minutes; gradually, both the back and the side grew nearer. There was nothing to grip, and Harvey could only wait until a downhill part of the road. Then he could use the same forces that were trying to throw him off to slide to the front.

His prayer was finally answered when the lorry hit another crest and began to pick up speed. Harvey's planted feet started to work against him as he slid across the smooth surface, gaining momentum. He turned mid-spin to slide feet first and slammed his boots into the roof of the cab. Harvey felt secure for the first time since the lorry had driven off with him underneath it.

Jimmy immediately leaned out of the window to identify the noise. His eyes opened wide in surprise when he saw Harvey stood above him. Jimmy's reactions were faster than Harvey expected. He began to slalom up the next hill, forcing the lorry from side to side of the narrow cliff road. But Harvey had handholds now. He stood above the driver's window waiting for his chance.

As soon as Jimmy leaned out again to see the results of his sharp turns, Harvey slammed his boot down onto his head. Jimmy's feet lost the pedals. The truck surged as it lost momentum and Harvey was thrown forwards. He reached out as he fell and just managed to grab hold of the huge wing mirror, then swung around to the driver's door.

Jimmy had barely recovered from Harvey's kick but was reaching across to the passenger seat for his gun. Harvey, half in and half out of the window, took a firm grip on his throat. A lorry coming the other way sounded its horn and threatened to hit Harvey's legs, which hung out of the window.

Keeping his grip on Jimmy, Harvey dragged himself all the way into the cab. Jimmy had the gun. Harvey pinned his arm to the seat with everything he had. Jimmy was fighting to control the lorry with all the commotion. Keeping his eyes on the road, he reached forwards and clamped his teeth into the back of Harvey's neck, biting down hard.

Harvey felt the teeth pierce skin. He slammed his elbow backwards into Jimmy's face. The truck immediately began to veer across the road. It scraped against the barrier that ran along the edge of the cliff, sending a shower of sparks into the air.

Taking hold of Jimmy's hand, Harvey snapped his fingers backwards with a violent series of cracks until Jimmy released the gun and screamed in agony. The weapon fell back to the floor of the truck, and Harvey began to pound Jimmy's face with his feet. The truck swerved violently across the narrow road, and the passenger side slammed into the rocks behind Harvey's head, sending shattered glass raining down on him. A deafening roar of jagged rock tearing at steel filled the cab.

Jimmy held one hand on the wheel. The other rested uselessly on his lap. Harvey took a glance through the windscreen and saw his chance; another oncoming truck approached. He straightened himself while Jimmy fought to steer to the lorry then rugby tackled him flat against the inside of the door, slamming his head against the hard interior.

Jimmy fought back with a headbutt then spat blood in

Harvey's face. Undeterred, Harvey grabbed Jimmy by the scruff of his neck and pulled him closer. Just as the oncoming lorry was about to pass, Harvey forced Jimmy's head through the open window of the cab and snatched the wheel to the left.

The force and violence of the oncoming lorry meeting Jimmy's head wrenched his body from Harvey's hands and sucked him from the cab, leaving Harvey alone to steer the lorry back onto the right side of the road.

He changed down a gear as he reached the top of the next hill then planted his foot firmly on the accelerator, giving it all he had. In the distance, and far below him on the cliff-side road, he caught a brief glimpse of the other truck.

Harvey had Melody firmly in his sights.

————

Once the first panel of the shutter door was off, the rest came away easily. Melody and Ladyluck each grabbed onto the top of the panel down and heaved backwards. The strips of fibreglass flexed, worked loose from the shutter mechanism, and then snapped away. Within a few minutes, they had a pile of broken shutter panels and gap large enough to step through.

"Are you ready to jump?" asked Melody, holding onto the side of the truck and peering out over the cliff that dropped down beside the road.

"Jump?" said Ladyluck. "I told you before I am not jumping from a moving lorry." She began to get agitated. "First of all, you want me to jump off a building, now you want me to jump from a moving lorry." She waved her hands in the air. "Where is it you're planning on jumping *to*?" she asked. "Have you seen the drop?"

"Ladyluck," shouted Melody, instantly silencing her

colleague. "Just calm down." She smiled at her friend whose face was frozen in a look of sheer terror.

"*Calm down?*" said Ladyluck. "You're *nuts*, Melody."

"You want to be rescued?"

"Of course I want to be rescued," said Ladyluck.

"Well, shut up then, and get ready to jump." Melody smiled at her and pointed at the half-destroyed lorry that was catching up fast. The right-hand side of the cab looked like it had been torn off. As the driver took the corner far too fast, the two women saw a streak of red down the driver side that ran the full length of the truck.

"Is that-?"

"None other," finished Melody. She waved Harvey closer, but the engine was already at its limit, issuing out thick smoke from under the cab. Harvey was catching up, but it was slow progress. Streaky must have seen the ruined lorry in his mirror because his driving suddenly became very erratic.

Harvey matched him turn for turn, and when Streaky slowed for a bend, Harvey just forced the lorry around at maximum speed, scraping the cliffs on the inside turns and the barriers on the outside as he closed the gap. With each bend, he grew closer and closer. The two women stood either side of the cargo bed, holding on tight to the remains of the shutter for stability.

Melody saw Harvey look at the road ahead. She could just make out his nod to her. Melody poked her head around and saw the downhill approach.

"Get ready, Ladyluck."

"What?" she cried. "No, Melody. No."

Harvey had closed the distance to just three metres. The engine screamed in revolt, and Streaky was giving his truck everything it had. With the flexibility of a dancer, Harvey brought his left leg up to the dash and began to kick at the edges of the windscreen. It shattered on the first blow, but Harvey lost speed with his efforts and brought his leg down.

Melody instinctively knew what Harvey was trying to do and drew her Sig. She waved it at Harvey and caught his eye.

He nodded once more.

She let go of her grip on the side of the truck, spread her feet shoulder width apart, and fired four times, placing a round through each corner of the windscreen.

"What are you doing?" shouted Ladyluck over the racket of the half-destroyed truck and the wind that rushed past. "You're going to kill him."

Melody tucked her Sig back into her waistband and watched as Harvey then forced the ruined screen out of its retaining rubber seal. With a final push, it fell away to the road below.

The pursuit came to an incline. Harvey saw it coming; he changed down to third gear and slammed the accelerator to the floor. Streaky hadn't been ready. He lost speed as he hit the hill, and the front end of Harvey's truck slammed into Streaky's rear end.

"Jump," he shouted. "Now."

"No way," said Ladyluck. She was truly terrified, gripping onto the side of the truck with everything she had.

Melody edged over to her.

"Quickly," shouted Harvey. He peered out of the side windows. "We're running out of time."

"Get away from me," said Ladyluck, seeing Melody grow closer, but refusing to let go of the side of the truck.

"Come on. There's no other way," shouted Melody.

Harvey slammed again into the truck, but Melody balanced like a surfer. She reached out to Ladyluck.

"No. You go," shouted Ladyluck. "I'll stay. I mean it. Go."

"If you stay, I'll stay," called Melody.

"I can't do it." She looked petrified.

Melody grabbed her arm. "Ladyluck, he's going to kill you."

The lorries rounded a bend and Melody lost her balance. Ladyluck grabbed onto Melody to stop her falling away. As the truck straightened, Melody yanked her off the side of the truck and held her from behind.

"I told you, I'm not leaving you behind again," Melody shouted into her ear.

"No, Melody, don't."

Harvey must have seen what Melody was doing, and once more closed the gap, slamming the trucks together. Melody used all her weight to pull Ladyluck down. She launched them both off the back of the cargo bay and in through the empty windscreen space.

They bounced off the passenger seat and landed on the floor of the truck in a sea of shattered glass with Ladyluck on top. Harvey looked even more determined and maintained his speed.

"Stay down," he called to them, and then dropped the gear once more. Ladyluck peered over the dashboard. Melody pulled up and joined her to watch as Harvey loitered a few meters behind Streaky with a sharp bend approaching fast.

"Harvey," said Melody. "We're not going to make it."

Harvey didn't reply.

"Harvey?"

He slammed the trucks together one last time, span the wheel left then right, forcing Streaky to counter his push. As Streaky tried to slow for the bend, Harvey gave the truck everything it had, forcing him to drive faster and faster towards the turn.

A harsh squeal of brakes sung out over the din of the engines. Burning tyre rubber joined the stench of hot oil and smoke, and Streaky's truck burst through the steel barriers and launched off the edge of the cliff in a final crescendo to the performance.

Harvey hung onto the wheel with everything he had. They slammed into the barrier, past where Streaky had broken through. In a shower of sparks and a deafening grinding of steel on steel, he finally coaxed the vehicle onto the road.

A tense silence followed. Both Melody and Ladyluck held on for dear life. Melody tried to look behind to see Streaky's lorry descend into the valley, but it was out of sight. It would be destroyed on the rocks below in a ball of flames, along with its driver.

13

ELEVATION

THE TRUCK LIMPED TO A STOP IN A SMALL COASTAL VILLAGE at the foot of the mountain range. It seemed to sense the end of its ultimate journey. The engine cut out without Harvey even touching the ignition key, and a great wash of steam rose from the engine bay.

"Oh, those poor people," said Ladyluck. "I do hope they're okay."

"Why don't you go take a look?" replied Melody. "Just give me a minute here with Harvey."

Ladyluck took the hint and disappeared towards the back of the truck.

"You okay?" asked Harvey.

Melody nodded. "I'm worried about Reg though. Ferez is going to be mad as hell about this. He might lash out."

"How's he going to find out?" asked Harvey. "As far as he's concerned, Derby and Barnet are dead, and you and Ladyluck are either dead or on the way to being dead with your mate Streaky. I've done everything he asked me to do."

"What happens if Ferez tries to call Streaky?"

"I doubt he'll be able to answer." Harvey smiled.

"He's not stupid. He'll know something's up," said Melody.

"Well, then we need to find them quickly."

"Sorry to interrupt your plans for world domination," said Ladyluck, "but there's a padlock, and I can't open the shutter door."

"It's okay," said Melody. "I'll help." She jumped down from the cab and walked with Ladyluck to the rear shutter. Harvey joined them. He always enjoyed watching Melody solve problems.

"Hey, Ladyluck," said Melody. "For the record, I'm sorry I threw you out the back of a moving truck. No hard feelings, eh?" She pulled her Sig and readied it to shoot the padlock.

"No hard feelings?" replied Ladyluck. "That was wild. It was the most exciting thing I've ever done."

Harvey smiled to himself.

"In fact," Ladyluck continued, "can I do *that*?"

"Shoot the padlock?" asked Melody.

"Yeah, can I do it, please?"

Melody offered the grip to her.

"I haven't fired a weapon since basic training, and even then, it scared the hell out of me."

"Okay well just keep-"

Ladyluck fired.

Bits of the padlock's mechanism scattered across the ground.

"Yep," said Melody. "Just like that."

Harvey shoved the shutter door up, and the three of them stared into the darkness. Sixteen eyes peered back from the shadows. They were bunched into the corner behind toppled boxes and scattered kilo parcels of greyish brown powder wrapped in clear plastic.

"Lower the weapon," whispered Melody, ignoring the drugs. "They're frightened."

Ladyluck did as Melody instructed.

Melody climbed up onto the back of the truck but kept her distance. "Come," she said. "You're free."

The refugees didn't move. They just huddled closer together.

Melody waved her arm to the open shutter. "Come." She smiled at them, but the scared faces with wide eyes remained where they were.

"T'aallu l'hon ma takhafu," said Ladyluck, peering into the truck and offering a large friendly smile.

The man in the middle raise his head. His eyes squinted.

"Come."

Ladyluck waved them over. "Intu halaa ahraa."

He slowly got to his knees and seven pairs of eyes all turned to him in wonder. The man took a few tentative steps towards Ladyluck.

"You're free now," she said, and waved her arm to present the tiny village.

"Ladyluck," said Melody, "I didn't know you spoke Arabic."

"I speak a few languages," she replied. "I think I've worked out what happens to *me* now. I've had my fun, and I don't think that coming with you is an option, even for the new adventurous Ladyluck. It's probably going to be dangerous, isn't it?"

Harvey nodded. "You're going to take care of these people?" he asked.

Ladyluck nodded. "It's what I do, right?" she said softly. "I take care of things. I'm a fixer, after all."

Harvey looked down at Melody. "It'll make it easier," he said.

"I'll get rid of the drugs, and find these people somewhere safe," said Ladyluck, pleased that she finally had something to offer to the operation.

Melody reached for her phone, found the number she was looking for and hit dial.

"Jackson, it's Mills. We hit a few issues. Find me Tenant's location and ping me the coordinates."

―――――

"An island?" said Harvey. "What is he, a Bond villain?"

"Many of them here are uninhabited but the local fishermen would know of them."

Harvey began to scan the coast.

"What are you looking for?" asked Melody.

"Well, I was going to steal a car to get back to Athens."

"Steal?" asked Melody.

"But now, we need a boat," said Harvey. "So we're going to steal one of them instead."

"Borrow, Harvey. We're going to borrow a boat."

"Call it what you like, Melody."

The pair dropped to the beachfront. Heading away from the village, they found one of the many small marinas that dotted the Greek coastline. They stopped a few hundred yards from the entrance.

"We can't just walk in there and take whatever we want, you know," said Melody.

Harvey didn't reply. He was eying the boats that were moored inside.

"You see anything you like?" asked Melody.

"Yep," said Harvey. "But we're going to have to swim for it."

"Swim?"

"Well, there's a dozen little boats in the marina that would serve our purpose. But there are too many locals about, they'd know who owned the boats. The last thing we want is for them to call the police. It would take some pretty good explaining."

"So?" said Melody, following Harvey's eyes. "You want to swim out to that little speedboat?"

"See any other options?" said Harvey. "The clock is ticking."

"Right, let's get it over with," said Melody, pulling her phone out and ensuring the waterproof case, which she kept on as standard, was secure. The Mediterranean was warmer than cold, but colder than warm. Fully dressed, the pair walked into the sea.

"What if someone sees us?" asked Melody.

"If you keep looking around nervously like that, they will. But if you act naturally, you'll be surprised at what people don't see," replied Harvey. "Swim around to the far side of the boat.

They reached the little Bayliner tied to a buoy a few hundred yards out, and hung onto the side. Harvey pulled himself up. His clothes and boots were heavy with water. He rolled onto the white and blue bench seat and then dropped to the fibreglass deck. Melody followed suit, anxious to see what he had planned.

"Now what?" she asked. "There're no keys."

Harvey gave her a look as if to question her confidence in him and then slid forward. "Just keep your head down."

He reached behind the console and pulled three wires from the ignition then ran each of them across the earth strip until he found the live wire, which produced sparks. Then he touched the live wire against the other two wires one at a time. Touching the first caused the ignition lights to illuminate. He carefully twisted the bare copper end together with the live wire then touched the twisted pair with the end of the third wire.

The starter kicked in. Harvey pumped the little primer

knob a few times, then touched the cables together again. The engine kicked into life and began to idle.

"I'm impressed. You didn't even have to destroy the boat," said Melody.

"An old friend showed me how to do it once before," replied Harvey with a smile. Then, staying low, he eased the throttles forward one click while Melody untied the rope to the buoy.

"You set?" he asked. "Don't look back. Act naturally."

Melody nodded.

Harvey eased the throttles forward a little more but stayed down low until they were far enough from the shore not to be identified. Melody slid forwards and took the seat beside him at the helm. She was smiling to herself.

"What?" asked Harvey. "What are you smiling about?"

"You," she replied. "You're such a criminal."

Once they were out of sight of the marina, Harvey gunned the engines. Melody enjoyed the views and guided Harvey, following the location that Jackson had sent through to her phone. The little sports boat skimmed the surface of the Mediterranean, leaving a wake that weaved between the islands.

"Dead ahead," called Melody over the loud engine noise. She pointed at a circular island in front of them. The land itself seemed to form at an angle, as one giant mountain rising from the depths of the ocean.

"There must be another way in," called Melody. "That's going to be impossible."

Harvey drove in a wide circle around it, seeking the best place to moor the boat at a safe entry point. On the far side of the island facing the sea, a small, welcoming bay enjoyed calm waters and rich sand. Inside, moored at the far end, was Ferez's boat. Harvey saw it, slowed, and steered the stolen Bayliner into the bay.

"You're just going straight in?" asked Melody. "Have you ever heard of stealth?"

"Reg and Jess are still alive, right? The team in London can see them here?"

"Yeah, they picked up the trackers," replied Melody.

"You don't honestly think that Ferez actually wants Reg and Jess, do you?"

"So why does he have them?" asked Melody.

"Because he knows *we'll* try and rescue them, Melody." Harvey drove slowly into the little, secluded bay towards Ferez's boat. Sheer cliffs rose up high on either side of them. In the centre sat a tiny beach. Behind it was a dense but small forest. It lay before the steep hills that rose up to meet the cliffs on either side, forming what looked to be a plateau.

"So, you think he wants *us*?" asked Melody.

"I do," said Harvey. "And if he does, coming in stealthily isn't going to help. My guess is that he'll be sitting up there hiding and waiting to take us out."

"So we're just going to walk into a trap, are we?" said Melody.

"No," said Harvey. "I'm going to walk into the trap."

"And what am I supposed to do while you do that?"

"You'll be figuring out a plan to save Reg and Jess, while I figure out a plan to kill Ferez."

Harvey tied off to Ferez's boat before the pair dove into the water and swam the short distance to shore. They reached the forest to the rear of the beach and began the steady hike up the hill.

"Is that the best plan you can come up with?" said Melody. "What happened to your mantra? Patience, planning and execution?"

Harvey stopped and looked up at the long scree slope ahead of them. Melody stared at Harvey's back as he rolled his neck from side to side with a satisfying click.

"You see that cliff up on our left?" asked Harvey, without turning around.

"Of course," replied Melody. She followed the veins and cracks in the limestone from the sharp rocks that stood like daggers in the sea below to the precipice that reached out three hundred feet above them like a child's bottom lip.

"Look closer," said Harvey.

———

It took the pair more than an hour to climb the steep scree slope up to the plateau. The island's terrain was scattered with loose rocks and wild plants that had somehow managed to take root in the deep cracks of the limestone.

At the top, the plateau led left and right. It seemed that the island had once been a volcano. One side of it had crumbled away, leaving the arc of a c-shape remaining and standing tall amongst the surrounding islands.

The two tiny dots on the edge of the precipice that Harvey had pointed out to Melody had been visible from below. But from the top, Melody couldn't see either of her friends.

The plateau was more than a hundred feet across in places. Deep cracks had long ago formed caves that led down to darkness, and sheer drops at the edges led straight down to the sea. Reg and Jess were nowhere to be seen.

The Mediterranean breeze was warm and strong at the top. Harvey, still topless with his shirt tied around his shoulder, powered on for a few more minutes.

"This is where we split up," said Harvey. "You go find Reg and Jess. I'll take care of Ferez."

"No, Harvey. What if he has a gun?" replied Melody.

"He won't," said Harvey. "This is more personal."

"Here, at least take my sidearm." Melody reached for her Sig, but Harvey held her arm.

"No, keep that out of sight," he said. "You need it more than me. I'll be okay."

Melody began to protest, but Harvey turned away. He climbed up onto a large rock that must have stood there for all of time, and then surveyed the wild, harsh landscape in front of him.

He glanced down at Melody.

"Are you still here?" he asked. "Go find them and stay out of sight. I'm going to finish this."

Harvey didn't wait for a response.

The wind began to pick up as the late afternoon sun sank lower to the picture perfect horizon.

"Ferez," Harvey called out. He caught Melody in his peripheral vision ducking out of view behind him. He heard her moving across the rocks to make her way to the end of the ridge. "Ferez," he called out again.

No reply came.

Harvey continued to scan the plateau. He could see why the place was uninhabited. It stood on the edge of the islands, bearing the brunt of the elements that came across Europe from the Atlantic.

"Ferez."

He knew that he'd feel a gunshot before he heard it, but Harvey was ready.

"You want me?" called Harvey at the top of his lungs. "Come and get me."

During a temporary lull in the wind, Harvey heard the faint chink of rocks hitting rocks as Ferez climbed out from his hole. Harvey watched Ferez's lanky frame make his way to the centre of the plateau.

"Is this where you want to do this, Ferez?" asked Harvey.

Ferez stared up at Harvey on top of the rock. "This is where I dreamed of doing this, Mr Stone."

"It's your choice," replied Harvey. He slowly climbed down from the rock.

The two men stood twenty feet apart on a hundred foot squared piece of flat land at the top of a three hundred foot cliff.

"For a man with such a reputation, it almost seems like the ideal place to die, does it not?" said Ferez.

"Is that why you want me, Ferez?" replied Harvey. "Because of my reputation?"

"Yes and no." He began to walk in a slow circle around Harvey. But Harvey knew Ferez was looking to turn him around to face the sun.

"Do you always talk in riddles?"

"No," said Ferez. "But there're so many reasons why you need to die, and killing you, Mr Stone, has been the dream of many men."

"You mean you're doing this for someone else?"

"Again, Mr Stone, yes and no," replied Ferez. "You've upset many people."

"Name one," said Harvey.

"You need to understand the consequences of your actions, Harvey. Did your father never teach you that? Oh, yes, that's right; you didn't have a father, did you?"

Ferez smiled and continued his walk. Harvey refused to turn to face him.

"You killed a man six months ago in Dubai."

"Crowe," said Harvey.

"Yes, Crowe. I watched the whole thing live."

Harvey didn't reply.

"But the consequences of your actions, Mr Stone, have left a lot of men out of pocket, and well, if you keep on following this moral compass of yours, then I'm afraid sooner or later one of those men will seek some sort of punishment."

"You did business with Crowe?" asked Harvey.

"No. Not Crowe directly, Harvey," said Ferez. He was behind Harvey now, but the distance seemed to be the same. "We have a mutual friend. And well, something you didn't know about me, Harvey, is that I'm a lot like you."

"We're nothing alike."

"I used to be like you anyway, Harvey," said Ferez. "But I evolved. Killing isn't a career, you know."

Ferez moved into Harvey's vision on his right.

"You see, Harvey, I know you think you're doing a deed, and everyone knows how good you are at..." He paused as if finding the right word. "Redemption. All you seem to do is implicate people."

Harvey didn't reply.

"You sign other people's death warrants, Mr Stone, and now it's time someone signed yours. Who better for such a task than me?"

"You didn't summon me here to help you then?" said Harvey. "You should have been clearer."

"Oh, I invited you, Harvey, because I wanted to see you in action. I wanted to see you take on the big boys, the team who have had your back all these years."

Ferez continued his walk in another long circle.

"You see, I saw you in action in Dubai, and I saw the aftermath of your attempt at *retribution*, as you call it. But I still doubted it. I just had to see it for myself."

"So let's do it then," said Harvey.

"What's the rush?" said Ferez. "Are you afraid your precious little Melody will be in trouble and need your help?"

Harvey didn't reply.

"I thought to myself," continued Ferez, "that when two monsters collide, the one who prevails will absorb the energy from the fallen one. Not in a magical or a godly sense, you understand. I'm not a believer myself. Are you a believer, Mr Stone?"

"In magic?" asked Harvey.

"Or the gods," replied Ferez.

"I believe in black and white," said Harvey. "Things are, or they aren't."

"So predictable. You're living a cliché, Harvey."

"*Living* being the operative word."

Ferez disappeared behind Harvey once more. Harvey stood resolute.

"So when I considered how it might feel to be the one to take down the great Harvey Stone, I also considered the power it would give me. Can you imagine the fear I would evoke in people, Harvey?"

"Not really, Fernando."

"I can," Fernando continued. "I thought to myself, if I were to take down the great Harvey Stone, where better for the two monsters to collide in a final epic battle than atop the highest peak around, and overlooking my beautiful Athens."

"Like a god?" said Harvey, mocking Ferez's warped sense of reality.

"Like a god." Ferez stopped in front of Harvey and turned to face him. "One of us will die here today, Mr Stone." He smiled with confidence. "Are you ready to die?"

14

THE HARDER THEY FALL

Melody knew that there was no arguing with Harvey when he had his mind set on something, especially when it involved revenge. She'd learned not to fight it a long time ago. So she ducked down behind the massive rock that he'd climbed up, and made her way along the edge of the plateau, where the cliff edge stepped down in a series of ledges before the sheer drop. By making her way along the ridge, she was able to stay out of sight.

Harvey called out in the distance for Ferez to show himself. She should have known that Harvey would never walk into a trap; he was too smart. But Melody also knew that Fernando Ferez had earned his bones as a young teenager, the same way as Harvey, and that he'd been a notorious face in the European scene. She had every confidence in Harvey, but if he fell foul to Fernando Ferez, neither she, Reg or Jess stood much chance of escaping, gun or no gun.

Melody put the thought to the back of her mind and set on the task of finding Reg and Jess. The ledge she was traversing seemed to grow narrower with each step. It quickly disappeared, leaving her searching for hand and foot holds to take her to a small platform protruding from the cliffside.

Being an experienced climber, Melody spanned the gap with four moves, keeping three points of contact with the wall at all times and letting her legs carry the brunt of her weight. The sharp limestone was brittle from exposure, but she found solid handholds and crossed the first gap in under a minute.

The second gap was harder.

The short and narrow ledge on which she stood once again quickly became nothing but space for her toes, and the cliff began to overhang. It was the lip of the rock she had seen from below. On the far side of the gap stood Reg and Jess, huddled together and clinging to the wall with barely enough room to move.

Reg saw Melody first. His face broke into sheer relief for a fraction of a second. But then he realised that they may as well be a thousand miles apart. The overhanging cliff between them was just too much. Melody read it in his face and desperation spurred her on.

"Melody, no," called Reg. "Don't try it. It's suicide."

Jess turned around, still clinging to Reg, and Melody saw the look of sheer terror in her red and swollen eyes.

"There must be another way," called Reg.

"How did you get there?" asked Melody, peering over the edge at the waves crashing onto the sharp rock below.

"He lowered us down on a rope," answered Reg.

The wind had begun to whip along the cliff face, pulling any loose grout and sand off the rocks into Melody's eyes.

"There's a rope?" she said.

Reg nodded and held up the loose end apologetically.

Jess broke into tears again, and she turned away, burying her face into Reg's chest. The girl was freezing and scared out of her mind.

Melody scanned the problem. She'd faced overhangs before, and there were plenty of handholds, but she'd never attempted a perilous climb before in her big heavy boots. With the added danger of a three-hundred-foot drop onto the rocks below, she'd only get it wrong once.

Her mind mapped the moves and she danced the sequence on the narrow ledge, fixing the prominent rock features and cracks in her mind. Then, putting all fear behind her, she reached out with her left leg and wedged her boot inside a deep crack.

"So far so good," she told herself.

Reg was calling out to her. But her concentration and the roaring wind muffled his voice.

Climbing shoes would allow the climber to feel the rock and use their toes to sense how secure the foothold was. But her boots gave her no sensation at all. Taking a firm hold with her right hand, she reached out with her left and placed her hand inside a crack just wide enough to take it but deep enough to swallow her wrist. She balled a fist and tested the hold with a pull.

She pushed off onto her left leg. Her balled fist held her body close to the rocks. Melody didn't stop. In one smooth motion, her right arm swung beneath her left. Finding a strong hold, she then brought her right leg across. Climbing, for Melody, was all about the flow and motion. Stopping the motion breaks the flow.

She switched legs and allowed her left to extend out to the next deep vein. It was a full stretch for her, but her boot connected well. In three more moves, she had made the overhang. The next combination left her with an arched back, hugging the concave shape of the rock. She placed her entire arm into a crack, found a hold inside, and tensed her muscle, which locked her arm and allowed her to lean out to look for the next grip. One more combination and Melody would be within reach of the ledge. But it would be the hardest challenge yet. The cliffside by Melody's feet undercut the overhang, and from her precarious position, she could see no more footholds.

She would have to hang.

The hand holds looked good. If Melody reached out with her left hand and grabbed the largest knot of rock she could see, her right hand could follow. It would leave her one chance to swing her legs up to the ledge. Then she would have no plan; she couldn't see that far. But she was already a few minutes into the climb and her forearm muscles had begun to tire.

"Reg," she called out.

"I'm here," he replied. He was on his hands and knees with one hand holding onto the rocks and one hand extended out to her. "I'm ready."

Melody gave him a quick look to catch his eye. Reg wasn't a strong man or a hard man, but right there and then, she knew she could trust him with her life.

———

The first blow came from Ferez, a sharp jab that cut through Harvey's defence and slammed into his chest.

Harvey took the hit in his stride and let Ferez dance around the space. He was obviously a boxer or fighter of some description. But Harvey knew that Ferez would have a weakness.

A wild roundhouse kick that Harvey easily ducked confirmed Harvey's thoughts. Ferez was a kick-boxer. The roundhouse was followed up with a straight kick to Harvey's head, which Harvey sidestepped before slamming his head into Ferez's face.

Undeterred, Ferez regained his composure and began his

footwork again. Then, with the speed of a cat, Ferez threw a combination of punches and kicks, the last of which caught Harvey in the side of the head and sent him reeling, with his ear singing a high-pitch wail.

Ferez didn't let off. The next blows came at Harvey's legs, perfectly placed kicks aiming to break Harvey's knees. Ferez was smart. As Harvey blocked the kicks, Ferez threw two jabs with his fists at his face. Both connected, and both felt like he had been hit with steel.

Harvey sized Ferez up. He was tall and lanky, but inside, there seemed to be an iron core. Ferez outreached Harvey easily. Longer legs and arms gave him a considerable advantage as well as being trained. Harvcy too had been trained to fight in several disciplines, which had resulted in him developing a style of his own. It was a mixture of judo, aikido and taekwondo, all rolled together and polished with the sheer animal instinct that can only be learned on the streets.

"Come on, Mr Stone," said Fernando, smiling at his clear advantage. "You're not living up to your name here. At least give me something to remember you by."

Harvey's legs were pounding from the several blows, and his ear was still ringing. He rolled his neck to the left and to the right, waited for the satisfying click, and then turned to face Ferez.

"I'm not giving you anything, Ferez," he said. "Why don't you come and get it."

As predicted, Ferez immediately set at Harvey with a series of high kicks. Harvey's eyes followed Ferez's feet as he circled through the air harmlessly in front of him. But with each kick, he grew closer. Ferez was pushing Harvey back to the cliff edge. Harvey began to take small steps back, blocking the kicks as they came then absorbing the body punches, and using the opportunity to land three hard blows to Ferez's nose in succession.

Ferez collected himself, wiped his nose and grinned at the blood on his cuff. "There we go," he said. "But I expected more of you."

Harvey didn't reply. He was watching Ferez's every move, and stepping back out towards the cliff as another series of kicks came his way. He was learning Ferez's technique. A pair of double punches, left then right, followed a series of kicks. The kicks were to lower Harvey defence; the body blows were to wind him or break a rib. Ferez had yet to throw a power punch.

The time was coming.

Another six steps to the cliff edge. He was close enough. Harvey made his first attack on Ferez, who ducked and weaved, avoiding each blow and replying with a sharp uppercut to Harvey's gut. Harvey sucked it up and waited for Ferez's second reply. It came as expected. But instead of dodging or moving, Harvey grabbed the arm and twisted it in one smooth motion. He pulled Ferez off balance and slammed the heel of his boot into the taller man's knee.

The knee buckled and visibly bent the wrong way, but it did not break. Harvey increased the pressure on Ferez's arm, despite him raining blows with his free hand into Harvey's head and face. Harvey lost count of how many times he was hit by Ferez's iron fist. He carried on twisting until he felt the pop of the bone dislocating and the grind of twisted ligaments.

Ferez cried out. He kicked furiously at Harvey, sending him to the ground just a few feet from the edge.

Harvey couldn't have orchestrated it better if he tried.

Ferez hopped up and down and shook the pain from his knee. His arm hung uselessly at his side. "Get up," he shouted to Harvey, outraged. "Get up so I can finish you."

Harvey pushed himself up on one knee, and Ferez, seeing his chance, came at Harvey with a kick to his head. But with

Harvey's arms raised in an attempt to block the kick, he was caught off-balance and toppled from his crouch. Once more Ferez came at him with relentless punches of his good arm. The punches came fast and strong, but Harvey absorbed them, reached out for Ferez's damaged knee and with one hand on the man's ankle, he slammed the heel of his hand into the knee joint. This time, he felt the crunch of bone and gristle.

Ferez reeled with agony. The blows to Harvey's head stopped as the tall man stood with his weight on his one good leg, and one arm hanging dormant. He raised himself to his full height to deliver the hardest punch he could. But Harvey reacted fast. With his core wound like a spring, he released and landed an uppercut to Ferez's groin, doubling the man over. Unable to balance on one leg and with just one arm, Ferez was going down.

Harvey seized the moment. He reached up, grabbing Ferez by his collar, and rolled back, planting his foot in Ferez's chest. He used the momentum to pull Ferez onto him. Then, with all his might, Harvey straightened his leg and sent the man over his head and onto the edge of the cliff. Ferez landed hard on his back, with his feet hanging in the air. His one good hand held fast with everything he had left to a fist-sized rock that was half embedded into the ground.

Harvey launched himself at Ferez, but it was too late. Ferez had heaved himself up, rolled, and pulled the rock from the ground. It swung in a wild arc at the edge of Harvey's peripheral vision and connected with his head with a thump that seemed to echo throughout Harvey's mind.

He dropped to the floor and let the shadows of unconsciousness envelope his thoughts.

―――――

The ledge was only five feet long and two feet wide, with a crumbling edge. Jess stood with her back to the cliff, her hands gripping the sharp rock and a look of sheer horror on her face. She tried to call out to Reg, but all Melody heard was the rush of the racing wind in her ears.

Reg took hold of Melody's belt and heaved her up on her count of three. With just the toes of her boots on the ledge and her back arched toward the overhang, Melody's muscles screamed at her to let go. But her tenacious mind told her to hang on just a few more moments.

She timed the final push with Reg's pull, and let go of the rock. For the longest of seconds, Melody hung out above the sharp rocks below, with only Reg to keep her from falling.

"Grab onto me," called Reg.

Her arms flailed and her fingers brushed over the rock. She'd lost her chance.

At the very last second, when balance had tipped the wrong way, and Reg had given her all he had to give, Jess bravely stepped from the safety of the rock face. She grabbed onto Reg's belt, and heaved him backwards, pulling Melody with him.

Melody regained her balance, and Reg was able to grab onto her arm. She fell onto him, and rolled to the cliff wall, her eyes wide, and her breathing sharp and short.

Reg's moment of heroism was over. He suddenly realised how perilously close he was to the edge, and slowly eased backwards to Jess, calming only when he felt the rock against his back.

Melody wanted to laugh or cry, she wasn't sure which, but she felt the emotions surging through her veins in the wake of adrenaline. The three were silent. No words needed to be spoken.

Then loudly, even with the wind, came the sound of somebody clapping. Melody twisted and looked up to the plateau.

Fernando Ferez stared back at her.

Melody's heart sank.

He smiled.

"I see that look of disappointment on your face, Melody Mills," he called out. "He was never going to live forever, you know."

Melody closed her eyes.

"Even the great Harvey Stone isn't immortal," continued Ferez.

"You evil bastard," hissed Melody. "What have you done with him?"

"Now, now, Melody, I think you have your own little predicament to consider before you go making life even more uncomfortable. Although, while I'm on the subject, I have to say, you're almost as predictable as Harvey used to be."

The words hit Melody hard.

Harvey used to be.

"You saw your friends in trouble and couldn't resist it, could you?" He smiled down at the three of them. "It's almost like leaving a trail of candy for a child to follow."

"So what?" said Melody, holding back the tears that seemed to burn the insides of her eyes. "What do you want with us?"

"You?" replied Ferez. "I don't want anything with you except to watch you die."

Jess began to sob and sniff.

"Why?" said Melody. She was having to shout to be heard above the increasing wind. "What have we done?"

"Oh, Melody, Melody, Melody," said Ferez. He began to pace the cliff above, a near vertical eight meters of sharp rock. "I explained all this to Harvey before he..." He smiled again. "Well, you know."

"No," said Melody. "No, I don't. Why don't you explain it to me?"

"He said you have spirit," said Ferez. "He said you'd be trouble and couldn't go quietly, even without your boyfriend to save you. You can't just accept death, can you?"

"Who said?" said Melody. "Your boss?"

"He's not my boss," said Ferez. "He's more of a partner."

"So while you're up here in the biting wind, I imagine he's at home in the warm eating his dinner? In Athens, is he?"

"Not that it matters, Melody, but London actually. We've been watching you all for quite a while."

"So now you have us. Why don't you come down here and finish us?"

Ferez laughed. "I don't need to come down there, Melody. Not when I have this."

He produced a grenade from a small knapsack. Melody noted his left arm was hurt by the way he held it close to his body.

"My favourite," he called down. With a smile, Ferez put the pin in his mouth.

"Wait," called Reg.

"Ah, Mr Tenant, you've been so quiet. I wondered when I'd hear some of your futile quips."

"What do you want?" Reg asked. "Immunity? I can arrange it. I can make you a free man."

"Think about it, Ferez," called Melody. "All of this will be behind you."

"It will be behind me if I pull this pin and blow my problems from the side of this mountain. So what's the difference?"

"We can guard you," said Reg.

"Reg, no," hissed Jess under her breath.

But Reg ignored her. "I can turn a blind eye to your operations, Ferez. I can even make you invisible." Reg stared up at him with defiance. He looked like a man who was used to bargaining for his life. But Melody knew that deep inside,

Reg, the computer whiz and all-round tech guru, clung to every piece of hope he could muster up.

Ferez was silent. He was considering the choice. Even the wind seemed to die down at the weight of Ferez's next words. "Nice try, Tenant. But I think I'll take my chances."

Melody felt her knees go weak. Her shoulders slumped as if the tension had held her upright and now gravity pulled at her limbs and organs.

"Goodbye, Miss Mills," said Ferez, and he pulled at the pin with his teeth.

Suddenly, Ferez lurched forward. Confusion spread across his face. Blood seeped from the top of his head, and his leg seemed to crumble.

Ferez fell to the ground out of sight above them.

"What the...?" Melody began. But before she'd even finished her sentence, the tired and grimy face of a timid young girl peered over the edge.

"Who the...?" said Reg. But before he'd even finished his sentence, the tired and bloodied face of Harvey Stone peered over the edge beside the girl.

———

"Her name's Bella," Harvey called down to Melody as he replaced the pin through the grenade's trigger handle. "She found me." He turned and smiled at Bella.

"Oh Harvey," said Melody, and buried her face in her hands. "I thought-"

"Well, I'm not. But you lot will be if that sun goes down," replied Harvey. "Throw me the rope."

Melody coiled the rope ready to throw to Harvey, swung it back and forth a few times judging her throw, then launched it. The rope uncoiled flawlessly and Harvey caught it but winced at his wounds. His shoulder was bleeding from

Melody's gunshot, his neck was sore from where Streaky had bitten him, and Ferez had left his mark in several places.

"Who's first?" called Harvey.

"I've tied Jess on. She's the lightest," replied Melody.

Harvey sat on the ground, planted his feet behind a large rock, and began to take Jess' weight.

"Bella?"

She turned to him. Harvey indicated with his fingers for her to watch Jess.

"Help her, and tell me when she is close, okay?"

Bella nodded. She seemed to understand English.

Jess came up easily, though she barely helped. Instead, she hung with her eyes closed, and when Harvey could pull no more, Bella had to help her over the edge onto the plateau. Jess rolled and scampered away from Ferez's body as if it might jump into life. Then she lay flat on the ground, exhausted with emotion. Bella untied the knot, pulled the rope off her, and lowered it down to the ledge.

"Ask them who is next," said Harvey in slow, simple English as though talking to a child.

Bella nodded and leaned out over the cliff top and called down. "Who is coming next? The man, he wants to know."

Harvey smiled to himself. Her English was excellent.

It was Reg who followed, seeing as Melody was the only person on the ledge capable of tying a bowline knot. Although he was heavier, Reg at least took some of his own weight and semi-climbed. Harvey could feel the tension on the rope rise and fall. Once again, Bella helped him over the edge and removed the rope.

Harvey had a hard time keeping the rope tight when the time came for Melody to ascend. She free-climbed most of the way, and it was only when she got to the top and one hand reached over onto the plateau, did she look up and catch

Harvey's eye. She gave him a look of gratitude then began to heave herself over.

Just as Melody was about to pull her legs up, Ferez's hand reached out. The movement caught Harvey off guard. Melody fell backwards off the edge, and the rope slipped through Harvey's hand. It burnt deep into his skin as he clamped his fist around the rope. Then he felt the line slacken. Harvey held it with all his strength, knowing that Melody had bounced off the ledge and was hanging unconscious in the air three hundred feet above the rocks.

Reg backed Jess away from Ferez as he began to stand, but Bella threw herself at him. Ferez caught her by the throat and threw her to the ground, where she rolled and curled into a ball.

"You're supposed to be dead," said Ferez, staring at Harvey with one hand holding the wound on the back of his head. The other arm hung loosely at his side. Harvey strained to hold onto Melody as Ferez began a slow limp towards him.

Then, Harvey saw Reg do something he'd never done before; he launched himself at Ferez. But it wasn't enough. Ferez didn't budge. He simply knocked Reg to the ground with the back of his hand and continued limping towards Harvey.

Harvey wrapped the rope around his left hand as many times as he could, and stood. But Melody's weight pulled him closer to the edge. He countered the pull and leaned away, using his weight to hold Melody.

"Now we both die," said Ferez, with his unwavering evil grin. He pulled the grenade from his useless dead hand, gripped the pin with his teeth then spat it to the ground with the finality and certainty of death. "There's no escape now."

Harvey backed away. He knew that as soon as Ferez released the trigger, they would all die.

"Jess, get Reg out of here. Go hide in the boat," said

Harvey, never removing his eyes from Ferez. Harvey edged back, taking the fight and potential explosion as far he could away from the others. "Run," he shouted at his friends, who stood there aghast.

"Let them go. But you cannot run, Harvey," said Ferez. His voice was tired as if he knew it was the end. "Just accept your fate."

Harvey doubled back past him, switching the rope to his right hand. He chanced a glance down to Melody who swung lifelessly on the end of the line.

"Melody," called Harvey, backing up some more. "You need to wake up."

"It's no use to try and escape, Harvey."

Through the tight rope in his hand, Harvey felt the ping of the first broken strand. He looked down. The sharp rock edge was cutting through Melody's lifeline.

He needed to act fast.

"Melody," he shouted again. But still, she swung with the wind and Harvey's movements. "Okay, Ferez," said Harvey. "You want to die? You want me to die?" He felt his chest rise and fall with the adrenaline. The veins and sinew in his arms and neck stuck out with the weight of Melody.

He took three deep breaths.

"Come and get me."

Ferez's grin seemed to lengthen and form an arc that cut deep into his face beneath his huge crooked nose. He took a step forwards.

Out of nowhere, a shape rushed past Harvey's dizzied sight, collided with Ferez's damaged leg, and took him to the ground. Bella held onto the hand with the grenade, holding it shut tight with everything she had. Harvey stepped forward to help, but she rolled onto Ferez's leg. He screamed loudly and rolled on top of her just inches from the edge.

Harvey lurched forward to grab Ferez, but seeing him,

Bella pushed with everything she had. She growled, finding her last morsel of energy, and shoved Ferez over the side. There was just time, the smallest fraction of a moment of acquiesce, before she too was pulled down with him.

She dropped from sight.

Harvey fell to the cliff edge, still clinging to the rope, in time to see Melody's swinging body beneath him and the explosion as Bella and Ferez hit the rocks below.

15

SERENITY

MELODY WOKE WITH THE GENTLE ROCKING OF THE SMALL waves that licked at the boat. The gentle vibration from the engine formed a rhythm that seemed to pulse throughout her body.

She opened her eyes.

The boat was being steered by Harvey. Reg lay on the floor and Jess stared down at her, smiling, with Melody's head in her lap.

"Ferez?" she croaked.

Jess shook her head.

"Dead?" Melody asked.

Jess gave a gentle nod.

"You okay?"

Jess broke into a great big smile.

"Well you clearly are," said Melody.

"Why don't you worry about yourself for a change?"

Melody closed her eyes again until she felt the familiar touch of Harvey's hand holding hers.

"Are we dead, Harvey?" she said, without opening her eyes.

He bent and kissed her forehead.

"Not for a while yet," he replied. "How are you feeling?"

"Like I fell off a cliff."

"We're nearly back on land. We'll get you checked out."

Reg, who had taken over steering the boat from Harvey, called out to her. "You had us all a bit worried there, Melody. It's not like you to miss out on the action."

Then it dawned on her; Melody tried to sit up and look around. "Where's the girl?" she asked. "Bella?"

Harvey didn't reply.

"No," said Melody. "That poor girl."

"It was her that took Ferez down," said Harvey.

Melody shed a tear for the girl who had saved their lives twice and eventually given her own.

"It's over, Melody," said Harvey. He looked out over the waves to the approaching ancient city of Athens glowing in the dimming sunlight. "We'll remember her."

———

At the boatyard, Ladyluck was waiting for them with a face full of smiles.

"I spoke to London. They tracked you," she said, as Harvey brought the boat in neatly alongside the dock. She hugged Reg and Jess as they stepped onto the deck. Harvey stepped ashore to tie the bowlines.

"Wait," said Melody.

Harvey stopped and turned.

"Hey guys, do you think you could give us a minute?" she said to the team. They nodded and began a slow walk to a waiting car that Ladyluck had arranged. Melody listened to Reg and Jess begin telling their story to Ladyluck. Their voices trailed off.

"You okay?" asked Harvey.

"I'll be fine," replied Melody. "I'm bruised, but nothing is broken, and my headache will go. How about you?"

"Not bad," he replied, "considering you shot me." He smiled at her.

"I was thinking," said Melody, as she made her way across the small deck of the boat to stand in front of Harvey.

"Sounds dangerous," he replied.

"Oh no," she said. "I was thinking I should probably make that up to you."

"It's a gunshot, Melody," said Harvey. "It's going to take some serious making up."

"That's what I thought." She reached up to kiss him.

Behind Melody, the reflection of the sunset sky danced in a slow and shimmering rhythm across the glittering evening sea. As the sun reached down to touch the horizon, the two forms melding into one, Harvey reached down and returned Melody's kiss.

They held it for the longest of moments then Harvey broke away. He'd forgotten how good it was to be with her.

"So what do you have in mind?" he said, beginning to fall in with her suggestions.

"Well, we have a boat, we're on the Med, and there's the most beautiful sunset I've seen in a long time right here. It seems like a good place to start our next adventure."

Harvey didn't reply.

END OF BOOK STUFF

Stone Game - Book Seven- Chapter One.

When the doors of Pentonville Prison closed behind Noah Finn and he smelled the fresh air, he knew that life on the outside would be harder than on the inside. At least when he was locked up, guards could lock him in, and encounters with other inmates who preyed upon men like him could be kept away, as long as Noah played the game and reciprocated the good deed when the time came.

It had only been three years since he walked as a free man and nothing much had changed, except the sky was blue and cars were newer and more modern looking. On the inside, Noah had developed eyes in the back of his head. An almost sixth sense of situational awareness was the result of an extremely difficult first three months. He'd been beaten, raped and forced to do shocking things to other men with the point of a sharpened tool in his ear as motivation.

On the train to his old home in Dunmow, Essex, he sat at the far end of the carriage where he could see the other passengers and anyone who came in from the next carriage. He would be ready. Something else he'd learned; it wasn't good enough just to know where everybody was, he needed to be ready to defend himself whatever way he could.

He sat and watched London slip by and give way to the green fields of the Essex countryside. It was the middle of the day and a few other passengers shared the journey with him. All of them were oblivious to the man who sat at the end of the carriage, and the terrible things he'd done.

Eventually, the train stopped in Chelmsford, where Noah disembarked and made his way to the bus station outside. It seemed an age since he'd been there, and he remembered it well, despite the local council's vain attempts to keep it looking fresh.

Standing waiting for the bus that would pass through his village of Dunmow, he felt vulnerable. He was aware of his appearance; his dirty old running shoes, tracksuit bottoms and an old leather jacket were all the clothes he had. His smarter jeans had been ruined on his first day inside when he'd been accidentally left alone with two other inmates. Maybe it had been a genuine mistake, but Noah thought otherwise. He knew it had been a chance for the guards to size him up, to see if he would be trouble, to see if he would fight back, cry or just take his punishment. Noah Finn had curled into a ball on the floor and taken the beating. He hadn't cried, it had all happened too fast; the tears had come when he was taken to his cell and left alone for the first time.

The bus arrived and Noah stepped on, glad to be somewhere relatively safe. He noted the cameras on the bus; they hadn't been there before he'd been away. It gave him a sense of security. He kept telling himself that he'd paid his penance, and he was now a free man. Yet he couldn't shake the feeling that society hadn't forgotten, and they never would.

The ride took thirty minutes, and Noah allowed himself a smile at the familiar sights. He made a plan. He'd pick up a few things from the store and then go home, where he'd stay for a few days. It would take that long to get his things together and his money sorted. Then he could leave, and go find somewhere he wouldn't be recognised. A new life was what he needed. A fresh start.

The bus stopped at the north end of the village, and Noah stepped onto the pavement. He habitually looked left and right and then behind him before he began walking at a brisk pace towards the big store halfway down the high street. He glanced over his shoulder and avoided eye contact with the few people he passed by looking into the shop windows. Thankfully, nobody recognised him.

He began to feel safer when he turned into his quiet street. His house was the third from the end, a semi-detached three-bedroom house that his parents had left him. A part of Noah was thankful that his parents were dead. They'd be destroyed by the shame. But part of him wished his mum was alive; he always felt safe with her. She had died a few years after his father, and as he walked along his street, he remembered how they'd sit together in the evenings. Noah had often been taunted by the local children for his appearance. He knew he had the look of a dummy, he knew his jaw hung open, and that his eyes were too close together. He knew his clothes weren't fashionable.

The kids had thrown stones at him and called him names. Some of it was because his parents were strict churchgoers and seemed to be stuck in the fifties or sixties. But he knew that he didn't help matters by the way he looked. One time, some boys had found him in the woods at the end of his street. It was the only place he could go to relieve himself when he got the urge. His parents wouldn't allow their son to molest himself in the house, and though he had his own room, their strong belief in God made him feel as if He was there, even though he secretly didn't believe himself. A stone had hit him on the back of his head, and he'd fallen over with his tracksuit bottoms around his ankles. That was when the taunting got really bad.

Noah's father woke up one morning to find the word 'wanker' sprayed across his old Ford Cortina, and people began to cross the street when Noah was walking towards them. Word had apparently gotten around the small village.

Those boys would be adults now, thought Noah, as he pushed the gate of his house open and closed it behind him. He wondered if they would remember him, or if it would all be put down to childhood shenanigans. He wondered if they'd still call him 'Nobby Noah' if they saw him. He didn't know why he cared what they thought or if they'd remember him. None of it would matter in a few days.

But he knew three girls who would never forget. He also knew that three girls meant three families, brothers, fathers and mothers who would all know sooner or later that Noah had been released. If he could keep his head down for a few days until his money came through from the transfer, he would be okay.

He stepped through the overgrown garden to the familiar brown front door, which now had flaky paintwork and abusive insults sprayed across the small glass window at the top. He shut the door behind him and leaned back onto it. Closing his eyes, Noah took deep breaths. He was safe.

He pulled the small security chain across to its locked position and let his eyes wash across the large hallway. The parquet flooring was just as he remembered it, dirty and dusty, but exactly as it had been. The flowery wallpaper his father had hung was peeling in some of the corners, and a simple wooden statue of Jesus on a cross was fixed to the centre of the wall between the front door and the entrance to the living room.

The house was large with huge bay windows at the front and a great chimney breast in the living room. The journey and his emotions had gotten the better of him and, seeing the couches in the front room, he realised how exhausted he was. He tested the lights; the electricity was still on. The bills had been paid automatically from his account while he had been away.

He sat down on the green couch and gently bounced twice, relishing the comfort. His mother's crocheted blanket hung over the back, just as Noah had left it. The TV wasn't a flash flat screen. It was big and boxy, and he had to stand to turn it on. He'd had a nicer TV in his cell, but not his mum's comfy green couch.

While he was up, he took his small bag of groceries to the kitchen. The huge butler sink stood empty, and his mum's pans and cooking implements hung on the walls all around it. The old gas stove seemed to have an angry face due to the position of the knobs and handles. The pantry door was closed. Noah knew it would be a mess inside. He knew the perishable food would either be stale or already eaten by whatever rodents had got in, but there would be tinned food. With the addition of the few items he had in his bag, he would get by for a few days.

"Just a few days," he told himself, smelling the musty, stale scent of his old home. Beyond the kitchen was the small glass conservatory his father had built when Noah was a boy. He recalled how he wasn't allowed to help in case a piece of glass fell and cut him in half. He also remembered that the conservatory could be looked into from the forest at the end of the garden. He wouldn't go out there.

It was a light summer evening, and he'd had a long day, so Noah ventured upstairs. He was looking forward to changing out of the clothes from the prison. Most inmates had clothes brought in for them. But those who either didn't have anybody or couldn't afford it wore the clothes they came in with or whatever was left behind by previous inmates. Noah had been given a pair of old tracksuit bottoms, which he'd taken to the shower room with him to wash.

The old bath taps gave some resistance, but eventually, after coughing and spluttering, and an initial brown offering, they had produced clean water, and it was hot. He let the water run and walked to his old bedroom. The bed was unmade but everything was as he had left it three years earlier. It was a mess. The police had turned the place upside down. It was as if they had known where to look. They'd found the girls' underwear beneath his drawer inside the cabinet, but had turned the place upside down anyway.

He stepped over the mess and pulled out some clean clothes and a towel from his cupboard. Then he stripped, wrapped the towel around himself and headed back to the bathroom. The bath was halfway full when he stepped in, relishing the clean feel of the water and the hot steam cleansing his body. Showers inside had been sparse and brief or had been long and painful if he timed it wrong. He was pleased to sit in the water, and a small guilty smile crept onto his face as he laid his head back and put his arms on the bath edge.

That was Noah's mistake.

It was fifteen minutes later when he tried to turn the water off that he realised he couldn't move his arms. They were stuck to the bathtub. He panicked and tried to rip them off, but whatever held him there began to tear his skin. He kicked the tap off with his foot and sat and thought about his predicament. He was confused. His skin was stuck by some kind of adhesive. But it was impossible.

Then he heard the voice outside the door.

Carry on with the adventure.
Click here to get Stone Game now.

ALSO BY J.D.WESTON.

The Stone Cold Thriller Series.

Book 1 - Stone Cold.

Book 2 - Stone Fury

Book 3 - Stone Fall

Book 4 - Stone Rage

Book 5 - Stone Free

Book 6 - Stone Rush

Book 7 - Stone Game

Book 8 - Stone Raid

Novellas

Stone Breed

Stone Blood (Available at the end of Stone Rage)

The Alaskan Adventure

Where the Mountains Kiss the Sun

From the Ocean to the Stream

.

A NOTE FROM THE AUTHOR

The Stone Cold Thriller series is set in East London and Essex and features places from my own childhood.

While many of the buildings, pubs and streets are fictitious, some of the more prominent locations in the series are borne from my own life experience and are as accurate as my memory allows.

My family are from Theydon Bois, where John Cartwright's house is located. In fact, my parents lived in the great house before I was born, renting a room off the wealthy owner, and I spent most weekends with various family members in the village. Theydon Bois is a very special place to me.

The headquarters building is based on the same road as my first flat in Silvertown.

In the first book, Stone Cold, the location of the first murder was in fact in the same building as my first job.

While the locations may offer an insight into my own childhood, and early working years, the characters are all fictitious. I recently handed the first draft of book one, Stone Cold to some family members and discovered that John Cartwright is, in fact, the name of my great-grandfather. I hope that he wasn't into the things the character John Cartwright is, and if he was, I'd like to know where the money went.

Stone Cold sets the scene for the rest of the series and is

the result of a considerable amount of research. I tried to understand what books were out there, what people wanted and, of course, what I wanted to write.

I do hope you've enjoyed the series so far, but more than that, I hope you've grown to feel for Harvey and the other characters, and if you've come this far, perhaps you'll come a little further and see how the next part of Harvey's story unfolds. I wish I could tell you, I'm itching to just blurt it out. But hey, where's the fun in that?

J.D. Weston

———

To learn more about J.D. Weston
www.jdweston.com
john@jdweston.com

GET J.D. WESTON'S STARTER LIBRARY FOR FREE

Do you want more FREE books?

I'm always keen to hear from new readers, so visit www.jdweston.com and find out how you can stay up to date on the latest Stone Cold news, plus get the J.D. Weston starter library for free, and get early bird discounts on all new releases.

ACKNOWLEDGMENTS

Authors are often portrayed as having very lonely work lives. There breeds a stereotypical image of reclusive authors talking only to their cat or dog and their editor, and living off cereal and brandy.

I beg to differ.

There is absolutely no way on the planet that this book could have been created to the standard it is without the help and support of Erica Bawden, Paul Weston, Danny Maguire, and Heather Draper. All of whom offered vital feedback during various drafts and supported me while I locked myself away and spoke to my imaginary dog, ate cereal and drank brandy.

The book was painstakingly edited by Ceri Savage, who continues to sit with me on Skype every week as we flesh out the series, and also threw in some amazing ideas.

To those named above, I am truly grateful.

J.D. Weston.

Copyright © 2018 by J. D. Weston

All rights reserved.

No part of this book may be reproduced in any form or by any electronic or
mechanical means, including information storage and retrieval systems,
without written permission from the author, except for the use of brief
quotations in a book review.

11357115R00113

Printed in Great Britain
by Amazon